BURY THE WOLF

BURY THE WOLF

The wolf does not speak our language, yet he knows our troubles better than we ourselves. He understands our thoughts, our fears, and our emotions. He sees our inner spirit and speaks with it as we sleep. Pray that it is a good wolf that finds you because sometimes, in the darkness, a bad wolf lurks.

Written by
James H Luker

This book is dedicated to my family. Thank you all for your love and support. Each of you are deep within my heart and fill my thoughts always. I greatly appreciate all the help in bringing "wolf" to publication.

A special thank you to A.G. for all your help in putting this together.

All biblical references were taken from The King James version.

Bury the Wolf

Preface

This book is a work of fiction and does not contain any real people or events. Many of the locations used exist but are used in a fictitious manner.

Chapter 1
THE LEGEND

"The old Indian had lived many years. He'd seen trees grow tall by the rivers only to fall, creating hurdles in the forest while giving broken branches for heat and shelter. He had watched his children play in and under snow-covered mountains then come to be buried in the valley below. The moon had risen countless times and the sun, even more. Men of lighter color, time and time again, came destroying his village, raping his women and taking his food. He was the last of his tribe and he had been alone for quite some time. With his death, with the end of his life, so too would be the end of the Charipou. The ancient warrior did not want this. His soul was strong, but his body was weak and feeble, scarred from great battles and pressing times of near starvation. Red, yellow, and blue ghosts danced above stacks of burning branches, revealing from the darkness an age-old face, covered with streaks from the crayons of nature. Oily strands of long gray matting hung from the peak of his loosely covered frame. The old Indian called out into the night praying for the gods to let his spirit live on."

A distant hand drum and chilling cries from ancient tongues emerged in the back of my mind as Professor Quartz brought the legend to life.

"The warrior had been chanting and praying for days for the gods to transfer his soul into the body of a worthy carrier. A surrogate, to pass on the heritage he was so proud to have been a part of. A body to carry on years of wisdom, centuries of knowledge, handed down from generation to generation. He knew his time was near. He prayed harder and harder as the hours and days went by. Tears, from exhaustion, pain, and heartache, streamed down his painted face."

"On the fifth day, just as all light from the heavens had gone, a massive red tail hawk swooped down from the black sky, letting out a great scream. As the chosen one lit on a huge boulder, the old Indian recognized what the gods had put before him and began to release his own spirit. But before the transfer was complete, a lone wolf jumped from the darkness and grasped the hawk. The ancient warrior, seeing what was happening, pulled a stone knife from his belt and thrust it into his own chest, but it was too late. The hawk had already received the Indian's spirit and the wolf had already devoured the hawk. He would not be allowed to climb high into the sky with the swiftness of a bird, with the knowledge of a warrior from centuries past, with an eye like that of an eagle, to watch over Mother Earth from above. Instead, the ancient warrior would be damned to roam the forest floor, in search of food to replace hunger, to burrow beneath the ground for warmth and safety, and to remain in fear of what he once was—man."

The legend consumed me the moment I heard it. Truth is, I was a sophomore in college, sitting at a cold hard desk, a little over halfway through the year. Vicariously, I was witnessing by the flame of a fire, a great warrior, who became a massive red tail hawk, who became a mangy carnivore, damned to roam the floor of the earth until man would inevitably destroy him. The legend went on to tell of how the Indian's soul would be allowed to live on for two more centuries. His spirit would pass from generation to generation, and his offspring would possess a spirit and knowledge such as that of his own. It was the legend of the feathered wolf. It was a legend that would become an obsession and eventually cost me my life.

"John…. John?"

I snapped to, looking up at Professor Quartz. I failed to see his long gray curly hair or his thick beard. Nor did I see the baggy cargo shorts and flip-flops that he wore every day, no matter the weather.

"Class is over. Are you okay?" He peered at me curiously through his thin round glasses.

"Yeah, I mean yes, sir. What was the name of that legend again?" I looked around to find myself the only student left in the room.

"The feathered wolf."

"Wow. It's... it's very consuming. Is it true or just made up?"

"True?" Professor Quartz hesitated a moment, "I would like to believe that it is, but then I would also like to believe that there is a higher intelligence out there. Don't you have another class to go to?"

"Yes, I do. Thank you." I grabbed my books and went about my way.

That night I sat on my bunk trying to remember the tale, word for word. I think I would have had a better chance if my mother would not have been so insistent on uncovering all the sad facts of my nonsocial life. Since the passing of my father, two years prior, I was almost guaranteed a weekly phone call from her inquiring about friends, girlfriends, social events, or possible dates. As always, my reports would disappoint her and, unfortunately, I didn't have any siblings to pawn her off on.

The truth is, among people, I didn't fit in at all and the move from rural South Carolina to college-town New York hadn't helped any. A large academic scholarship and a promise to my dying father were the things that had brought me to this concrete hell, and the promise was the only thing keeping me from going home. In some ways I made an extra effort to fit in, but for the most part I withdrew further and further into myself.

In the following weeks, my desire to know more about the feathered wolf kept me very busy. I searched every library, bookstore, and website available. Information on wolves in general was overabundant. The feathered wolf, however, was proving to be a very elusive creature. On many occasions, I probed Professor Quartz on the subject, but he seemed hesitant to give me any more information. Maybe he had already told me all that he knew. I don't know if I was about to lose interest or just getting extremely discouraged when I finally ran across an old newspaper article that would, in time, lead me to these mystical creatures.

I read aloud, "Charipou Indian artifacts discovered on Isle Royale." Clumsily bumbling from my chair, I jumped up to retrieve a map. Everyone in the library quickly flashed hateful stares for the disruption. "Isle Royale, Isle Royale, Isle Royale," I whispered lowly, frantically searching a large map tacked to the back wall. "Canada! Lake Superior! Yes!" I could not help but yell out as the tip of my finger found the isolated engulfment. It looked to be a very large uninhabited island almost a thumb's width south of the Canadian border. I felt, at last, I was onto something. After much research, I had finally found a lead toward this almost unheard-of tribe. The article did not say anything about the legend, or wolves, but it did state that this was believed to be the last territory occupied by the Charipou after being driven north by the civilized world. According to the article, several hand-dug copper mines and earth-covered camps were discovered along with hundreds of Charipou artifacts in June of 1950. I had found in previous research that wolves did currently inhabit the area also. Everything seemed to be falling into place. Carter, my Zoology instructor, had just given us an assignment to do an up-close and personal observation of any animal not living in captivity. This was to be turned in after spring break. With any luck, these wolves would be my subject. Smiling, I held a copy of the article up to the burning sun as I made my way to my small apartment.

After darkness fell, a voice called out in my dreams. The spirit of the wolf whispered in my sleep. Sounds of an ancient tongue echoed in the back of my dormant mind, calling me to their world. It seemed that the wolf was also hunting me. Not for the kill, but for the capture. Throughout the night, their pursuit was relentless. Ghostly images of Charipou Indians blended with the bodies of flying hawks circling above burning branches and dancing wolves. A ritual was taking place.

The next day, I could hardly wait for Professor Quartz's Anthropology class. He and I both shared an undying interest in the feathered wolf. Maybe because of my youth I displayed much more enthusiasm, but Professor Quartz seemed just as interested, and I had a hunch that there was more that he had yet to share with me.

As soon as class was over, I approached his desk with a feeling of supreme achievement. When I placed the article in front of him, he took only a moment to look at it then leaned over to open a drawer beside him.

"Did you see?" I questioned impatiently. "Did you see what that was?"

When he righted himself, he tossed an identical copy over the top of mine, then smiled. "I've been keeping that for years."

"Why didn't you tell me?" I asked.

"What? You think that I should just give you hours of research? I don't think so.... No, really, I dug it out of the attic just a day or two ago. I was waiting for the right time to show you." Professor Quartz stood, stretched, then opened a window, leaning onto the sill. "You know, at one time in my life, I tried to follow up on this myself. About ten years ago, I was fifty-five, maybe fifty-six, I had everything planned out." Professor Quartz stood silent for a moment.

"What happened?"

"I was hit with prostate cancer and nearly died."

"Whoa, sorry to hear that. Why didn't you go after you were well?"

"It took a long time to get myself back. I could hardly climb the stairs in my apartment. Isle Royale is rugged, very rugged, and heavily forested. The chance of even spotting a wolf would be slim. And how would I even know if it was one of them? I guess I just lost my drive for such silly things." Professor Quartz coughed to clear his throat. "Yes, I had it all planned out, even down to the food I would take. I guess it's silly for a grown man to go chasing such a foolish thing, but I've got to admit the legend still intrigues me."

"As it does me… as it does me." I spoke in a low monotone voice, slowly nodding my head.

I wanted to tell Professor Quartz about what I had in mind, but for some reason I thought it best that I didn't. Maybe I felt like he would think less of me to actually follow up on something he had just described as "silly." I knew in my heart, if I could just get one glimpse of these mystical creatures, I would have to share my experience with him. After all, he was the man responsible for sparking an interest in me that was quickly becoming an obsession. I made up my mind, as I walked from his classroom, that I would tell no one until my return. I did not want to have to deal with any criticism, and I definitely did not need any support or encouragement to embark on such an adventure. Alone, I would complete my mission. Alone except for the persistent haunting in my mind.

Chapter 2
THE FLIGHT

Spring break finally came, after two restless weeks of forever. Most of the students from school had been planning parties, road trips, and family reunions. I had been preparing for the adventure of a lifetime. Every bit of information I could find on Isle Royale wolves was studied thoroughly. I packed enough food for the trip and a small handheld water purifier for drinking. I also read about marten, mink, otter, red fox, and many other animals that were said to be inhabitants of the two-hundred square mile water-bound wilderness. Soon, I would find out firsthand. My camping gear and supplies were placed beside the door, steadfast and waiting for tomorrow morning's flight. My camera and journal would be backpacked throughout the trip. I did not want to take a chance on missing any entry due to these items being stowed away in the belly of a plane. My alarm was set, checked, then checked again.

At seven a.m., I awoke to what I usually considered an annoying buzz and by seven thirty, I was on the curb flagging a taxi down. "Where to?" The driver asked.

"The airport." I slammed the door a second time as we pulled away.

"Yeah, she sticks a little." He took a sip of coffee then turned his attention to the heavily congested traffic.

An hour later, I was at the airport, awaiting departure to Duluth, Minnesota. As I sat patiently, it came to my attention that this was the first time I'd experienced complete independence since leaving South Carolina. Back home I regularly disappeared, backpacking into the hills for as long as time would allow. There was no doubt that I was a loner and a lover of the forest, with all its creatures and mystique. This break from the concrete world was well overdue for a man like me. I had always possessed a special relationship with nature, and it was nice to think of the upcoming reunion. I did not know what I would find in my search for such an elusive animal as the feathered wolf, but I knew just to be in a peaceful and natural environment would be replenishing for my soul. I needed this almost as much as food and water, maybe even more.

"Flight four twenty-three, now boarding." The announcement echoed from the airport intercom. Three announcements, prior to this one, had been made concerning flight four twenty-three: "Flight four twenty-three has been delayed until further notice," they'd all rung out. This delay had put me behind on getting to my destination as planned, but I hoped that things would smooth out from here. I could only hope Lake Superior Bush Flights would be understanding of the situation and squeeze me in on a later buzz across the water.

Taking my seat on the airplane, my heart began to race. It wasn't from the excitement of the trip or the thrill of the flight. It was because of fear. This would be the first flight I had ever been on. I was trembling, sweating, and very, very jumpy. "I think I need air," I mumbled to myself.

"Sir, are you okay?"

"My gosh! You scared me to death." I grabbed my chest as a beautiful, bright smile came into view.

"First time?"

"Yes. How could you tell?" I raised my eyebrows in a cute puppy fashion, while asking a question we both knew the answer to.

"I'm Candance." A young flight attendant extended her hand forward, encouraging a formal greeting. Candance was beautiful, with deep green eyes and a light complexion. Blonde wasn't her natural color, but no matter what her dark roots thought, it fit her very well. She was petite, not too big in any area, but definitely not too small.

"John, John Ryder." My hand met hers.

"Well, John, you have nothing to worry about. I ride these birds just about every day and I'm still here.

"How long have you been doing this?"

"Two years, last month. You just settle in and relax. I'll come back and check on you in a bit."

Candance's words were very comforting for a while; that is, until I felt myself shoved into the back of my seat. Distant buildings, other planes, and the stripes on the runway were all going by at a rate of speed I considered much too fast. The sweating and palpitations started again. I had never been so nervous in all my life.

As soon as the plane reached cruising altitude, Candance was back with that same bright smile. "How are you doing, John?" She eased into the vacant seat beside me.

"Ugh," I rubbed my stomach.

Candance laughed, "I knew you would be just fine. Where are you going?"

I had to take a deep breath before I could find the words to answer her, "Isle Royale."

"What's there..., family?"

"No." I was trying to loosen up, but things were still shaky. "Wolves... I'm doing a study on wolves over spring break."

"Wolves, they still exist?" Candance gave a confused look. I don't know if she really believed that wolves were actually extinct or if this was just an effort to continue conversation in hopes that I would not lose my lunch all over her workplace.

"On Isle Royale, there are no people, just wolves... and other animals of course." Her eyes met mine as I gave a small smile in reference to her innocence.

"It sounds dangerous. What if you get eaten?"

"Well, would that be so bad?" I replied.

"You're bad, mister!" A promising glance was given as she stood, running her hand along her thigh to straighten her skirt. "I'll be back in a bit."

I smiled, not taking my eyes off her until she was

obscured by the seats in front of me.

Candance didn't come back until the plane had landed an hour later. Maybe I was too forward, I thought to myself, or maybe she was just doing her job, comforting a passenger. "See, I told you that you would make it."

"You know, I really wasn't afraid. I just wanted a reason to talk to you."

"Well, Mr. Ryder, dinner would be a reason to have this conversation you so desire."

I was taken by complete surprise. "Are you... asking me to dinner?"

"Yes. I hope you're not one of those old-fashioned guys who thinks a girl can't ask a guy out." A stern glare held steady for a moment but was soon replaced by a playful smile that spread slowly across her face.

"No... no, not at all, we can certainly do dinner." We smiled at each other for a moment; unfortunately, a moment that gave me too long to think. "Wait! I've got to check on my bush flight." I took another glance at my wristwatch. "I've all but missed it and I'm not sure when they'll be able to fit me back in."

"Tell you what, there are pay phones by the baggage claim. I'll be by there in about twenty minutes. I hope to see you." Candance walked away. I hoped it was not the last time that I would see her, but the wolves were priority.

I nodded my head then rushed from the plane.

A harsh, grumpy voice answered after the fifth ring, "Superior Bush."

I spoke quickly and clearly, "Hi, my name is John

Ryder. I've missed my flight with you guys from a… layover in New York. I was wondering when you could reschedule me."

"Flight was today?" The response was deep, congested, and to the point. I wasn't sure if the sounds were coming from a disgruntled old man or a large woman who'd smoked too many cigarettes for too long.

"Yes, two o'clock, Isle Royale."

The line was silent for a moment, except for the very recognizable sounds of loose papers being shuffled over what was probably an extremely cluttered desk. "John Ryder," was mumbled a time or two. "It'll be Wednesday at one."

"What? That's three days from now!"

"Sorry, bub. That's the best I can do. Take it or leave it."

Sincerely sorry he, she, or it wasn't. I shook my head in disbelief. "I guess I'll have to take it. What choice do I have?"

"Okay, Wednesday it is." Click! No "good day," no "goodbye," just a click.

"What a way to start the trip," I sighed. I was already pressed for time, and this would make the project nearly impossible. I thought for a moment about giving up, but it wasn't in me to just quit like that. I was raised to be strong and "press on," as my dad used to say. To look back on a situation and be able to be satisfied with my efforts, no matter the ground gained, was important to me. I tried to think positively. I knew a few days in the small town of Grand Portage would have to be better than time on the concrete plateaus of New York. The only real difference between being stuck in Duluth and the Big Apple was Candance and being a lot closer to crossing Lake Superior.

"John." Candance had approached me unnoticed. "What's it going be?"

"Looks like I'll have plenty of time to spend here in Duluth. Hell, I may even be able to save my money and hitch hike to Grand Portage."

Candance laughed out loud, but I wasn't joking. "There you go, that's looking at the bright side. And if you'd like, you can save on a room, too, and just bunk with me tonight."

I said to myself silently, "Press on.... Thanks, Dad." I didn't have to respond to Candance verbally; the small smile and slow nodding told her that I would be hers for the evening.

We had dinner and drinks at a very nice establishment, then retired to the room for an extremely passionate night. We held each other close and slow for hours. Later, we pulled the balcony curtains back and gazed shamelessly at the stars, clothed only in each other's arms.

But the wolf... despite Candance's presence, the wolf still hunted me. During my slumber, a hand drum played while a secret voice whispered, "boom boom, wolf." The sounds were growing stronger while my flesh was getting weaker, giving in to the spirit of the dark. My mind was becoming a lair where another lived; one that was definitely there, but one I could not yet begin to explain or understand. Throughout the night, the spirit of the wolf pulled at me with all of its lure and seductive witchery. My soul was being overpowered.

Early the next morning, from under the covers, I silently watched Candance dress and leave, returning to her job. I didn't think of her as bad in any way. I saw her as a beautiful, passionate woman who lived her life the best she could. Whether she liked it or not, her job forced her to forfeit most commitments and long-term relationships. She could have nothing of sensual pleasures, or one night, string-less stands as she ventured from city to city. I could not help but to think that a woman with this much desire would shrivel up and fade away behind the confines of abstinence. She meant to leave me sleeping but left me awake with a feeling of warmth and awe, having experienced her beauty. Even though I knew I was just a small moment in her life, I felt very fortunate to be just that. I whispered, "Goodbye, beautiful," as the door slid from her fingertips, closing behind her.

After a long hot shower, I stood alone on the concrete balcony in a towel, sipping a cup of coffee. I took in a deep breath of morning air then let it go, yelling to the city, stories below, "This is going to be a great day!" After dressing, I grabbed my gear and walked to a nearby truck stop for breakfast.

"Good morning." I was simultaneously met with very friendly greetings from two waitresses.

"Coffee?" One asked.

I nodded in acceptance, "Good morning to you, too."

After taking a seat at the bar, I piped up. "I'll have two eggs and toast."

"Scrambled?" A waitress with the name tag, Liz, and a very wide frame questioned.

Taking scrambled to be the norm, I answered, "Yes, that'll be fine."

"Where are you going with all that camping gear?" Liz nodded toward my overstuffed backpack then scratched at the base of a gray ball affixed to the top of her head.

"Grand Portage, I hope. Then from there, Isle Royale."

"Looking for some alone time?" Liz asked.

"Yep, but my flight got screwed up, so I've got a couple of days to get there." I took a sip of the steaming coffee Liz had placed in front of me. "Think I may try hitch hiking." I smiled from behind the cup.

"We get a lot of that through here." Liz answered then pointed to a customer, two stools over. "Roy's going that way this morning in his big rig. You could probably catch a ride with him.

Roy was as trucker as a trucker could get. Sleeveless flannel covered his torso, and faded jeans, which had to be on their fifth day of wear, supported a chain-driven wallet and covered most of his lower portion. In dire need of a shave and shedding a few pounds, Roy looked at me, grumbling, "Be aw right with me." By his accent, choice of such few words, and his rebel flag/bulldog tattoo, it was obvious that Roy wasn't from Minnesota. A dirty old cap covered most of his shaggy red hair.

17

"Mississippi?" I questioned.

"Alabama, heart of Dixie. Why the livin' hell I came up here to this damn cold place is beyond me. You'd thank' a sum' bitch would have nuf' sense to get where he could at least stay warm."

"Now, Roy," Liz topped his coffee off. "You know why you stay up here, and you would think that after fifteen years you'd be okay with the cold." Liz looked at me, smiling. "He stays up here because of my baby sister, Katrina… And here she comes now." Liz's face lit up as the glass door swung open.

"That's Katrina?" I mumbled to myself with surprise. She looked nothing like Liz. Very slim, really too slim, and tall. She had well-groomed hair that touched her waist, even when Liz lifted her for a big hug. Autumn brown was the color, highlighted with a flickering reflection of sunlight that penetrated through the partially opened blinds, as the two swayed back and forth. Katrina looked as though she could have been attractive in her younger days. I got the impression that "hard" would describe much of her past. I found her ass quite attractive in jeans that looked as though they were pressed on. She was slightly lacking up top, but if she had been any bigger, she probably would've looked out of proportion considering her slim physique.

Liz pointed at me. "This gentleman may be riding to Grand Portage with you guys."

Katrina looked me over, then popped her gum. "Okay," she extended her hand softly. "I'm Katrina."

"John," I introduced myself. "I hope it won't be any

trouble, me riding with you guys."

"Oh no, not at all; Roy and I love company. We do that same old boring trip four times a week. It'll be nice to break it up. Isn't that right, Roy?" She nudged Roy with an elbow while running a hand across my shoulder. "It'll be fun."

Normally, actions like that would've made me uncomfortable but, at the moment, I just thought her to be extremely nice. "Well, if you guys will excuse me, I'm going to go to the restroom while Roy finishes his breakfast. I'll finish mine on the road, if that's okay?"

"Okay with me," Katrina popped her gum once again.

As I stepped up to the urinal, an elderly black man, who had been seated behind me in the restaurant, took post at the urinal beside me. Only our lower portions were hidden by a small, ragged partition littered with profanities and vile drawings. "Grand Portage, you say?"

"Yes, sir." I'm sure I displayed some nervousness in my voice, and I was very cautious to keep my eyes forward. I've never been comfortable with conversation during urination.

"Son, I don't like to pry in other people's affairs, but I'm afraid that you may be about to get yourself in a pickle."

I turned to look at him then quickly snapped back, locking my eyes onto a thin moldy strip of caulking that separated the small yellow and green ceramic tiles in front of me. In my quick erratic glance, there was time enough to see that the man had obviously tried to take care of himself over the years. He had kept himself trim and neat

19

except for the short gray whiskers protruding from his face. There were several bumps around both of his eyes, but they looked like they had been there for a very long time. He was dressed in black from head to toe. "What do you mean?" I asked.

"Katrina is a man... or used to be anyway. And Roy, well Roy's a very troubled person. If I'm judging you right, you don't want anything to do with them."

"You've gotta be kidding me."

"I wish I were. I've known the both of them for quite awhile. I can't understand it, but I guess... to each his own." He reached forward to flush.

"You're serious, aren't you?"

"As a heart attack."

"Oh, Lord, mister, you don't know how much I appreciate you telling me this. I should've known things wouldn't fall into place this easy." I shook my head in disbelief. I had completely let go of my embarrassment. I held my hand over the partition, "John. I'm John." The man smiled oddly as I realized what I was doing. Quickly pulling my hand back, I apologized. "Sorry."

"That's okay. Good news is, I'm on my way to Lutsen. That'll get you about forty miles or so from Grand Portage. That's if you don't mind riding in Sweet Pea."

"No, no, I don't mind. Wait, what the heck is Sweet Pea?" We rinsed then dried our hands on a few rough paper towels; the brown ones.

"You'll see, and it's Taylor. My name is Taylor."

Roy and Katrina both glared at us oddly as we walked

20

back from the restroom. "You know guys, I appreciate the offer, but on second thought I think I may stick around here another day. I've got plenty of time to get to Grand Portage and there's probably a lot more to do here in Duluth while I'm waiting for my bush flight."

"Ah, honey come on, you don't want to stay here." Katrina was obviously disappointed.

Roy sat silent for a short period then looked at Taylor with suspicion. "I guess you had something to do with this?"

"The boy's straight, Roy. Just let him go about his business." Taylor spoke sternly.

Once again, I was starting to get very, very nervous and unfortunately, I did not see any beautiful stewardesses coming down the aisle to comfort me. This is not how I wanted things to go. I thought I would just be able to change my mind about riding with the two and slip away, never to be seen again.

Roy stood from his chair, speaking gravely. "Me and you's got us a problem now, old man." Roy stretched tall, trying to intimidate Taylor with his size.

Taylor calmly unzipped his old leather jacket, easing his hand in along his chest. "You know what I'll put on you. Now sit down!" he demanded. "Get your stuff, boy, and let's get out of here."

Roy, obviously frustrated, did as Taylor said. Everyone else in the restaurant sat silent, trying to avoid eye contact with anyone involved in the volatile affair. I gathered my belongings, then Taylor and I quickly walked out. Thankfully, no one followed us. I think if they had, I may have run all the way to Grand Portage.

"That's Sweet Pea." Taylor pointed into the distance with a very full, large round key ring in his hand. We both nervously checked over our shoulders while making our way through the parking lot.

In amazement, I hesitated in my steps for a second as we came close to the radical ride. Sweet Pea was no average vehicle. She was an early sixties undercover police cruiser, completely blacked out with the exception of the blinding chrome rims, wide white-wall tires and a shiny, silver spotlight that rested just forward of the driver's door. Everything else was solid black.

"Wow, a classic, no doubt." The sight of Taylor's car encouraged me to temporarily forget about the trouble behind us.

"Yes, I've had her since the day she was issued to me." Taylor gleamed.

"You're a cop?"

"Was. I retired after thirty years. Oh, I still listen in on my scanner, carry my badge and gun. I just can't give it up. There are some things a man just can't do without; like breathing, food, women..., and living. Things were a lot different in my day. It was a respectable job, and most people were respectable too."

The heavy steel doors creaked and popped as we opened them. The interior of Sweet Pea was no surprise. It completely matched the exterior except for the fuzzy handcuffs over the rear-view mirror. The sight of them made me hesitate once again. For a short moment I wondered if Taylor was the one I should be watching out for and Roy and Katrina were actually okay.

Taylor fired the rumbling engine. Sweet Pea sounded as though she were ready to race or ready to die. To the untrained ear, it's hard to tell the difference between the lope of a finely tuned racing engine and the miss commonly found with old junk vehicles. It was evident from the fumes that the exhaust system was not completely intact.

"Hurry up! Get in before she fills up with bad air and kills us both." Taylor patted the accelerator a time or two, keeping the old battle wagon alive.

I could see that Taylor was a good man. There was an aura about him, displayed by his enthusiasm and gratification even in the simplest of things. As I shut the door behind me, I felt ashamed for thinking otherwise. We rattled from the parking lot, leaving a slight tinge of smoke suspended in the thick morning air.

"I guess those guys know you used to be a cop."

"Yeah, I've known just about everybody in that diner for half my life. And they know I got my gun right here, too." Taylor tapped his chest then laughed contently. "But what they don't know is that it hasn't been loaded in ten years…. and don't you tell them, either."

I joined him with a good laugh in his self-contentment. I imagined that this incident would fuel Taylor's tank for quite some time. "Oh, God!!!" I yelled out, leaning forward as though I were going to puke.

"What?!" Taylor swerved nervously, looking at me as if I had lost my mind. "What's wrong with you?"

Putting my hand over my mouth, I gagged a bit. "I

thought Katrina had a nice ass."

"IIIIIII!" Taylor yelled out like a wild drunk man while beating the steering wheel. "You thought? IIIII--ha, ha, ha!" The beating stopped while he was actually speaking, then resumed, coinciding with the laughter.

"You're crying, Taylor! Come on, it's not that funny." I knew it was, but damn, I hated to have this one hanging on me.

"Yes, it is!" Taylor continued to laugh, beating the wheel intermittently. "And you know what the best part is? You got to live with it the rest of your life." Taylor wiped the tears from his eyes while continuing to laugh. He would get quiet then another outburst would overtake him. Red-faced, I couldn't help but laugh along with him each time.

After several more minutes, Taylor regained himself. "At least you didn't touch it." A large devious smile spread across his entire face.

"Or worse," I replied.

"What are you doing here, anyway, besides going camping?" We rumbled our way north, toward Lutsen.

"I'm going to study wolves on Isle Royale."

"Wolves!" Taylor exclaimed. "Don't you know they'll bite you?

I closed my eyes, shaking my head. "No, no. I'll be lucky to even see one. Wolves have been hunted so hard for the last hundred years, they run at the sight of a man."

"Yeah, run at you." Stressing "at," Taylor had the same preconception about wolves as most everyone else in the world.

24

"You've never touched a wolf, Taylor?"

"Oh, I touched one, one time with the front of Sweet Pea. He almost got away, but he wasn't quite fast enough."

A knot tightened in my stomach. I knew Taylor was a good man, he just believed the things he had been taught. "Let me ask you, Taylor. In all your years of being a law man, have you ever seen a wolf attack a person?"

Taylor sat quietly for a moment, driving. After thinking back through the years, he answered, "You know, I don't think I have. But you're not going to change my mind. And I'm most certainly not going to try and pet one."

I laughed. "Trying to pet one probably wouldn't be a good idea. Preserving one, on the other hand…." I didn't complete the statement. Sometimes I think a suggestion can be stronger if it's left open ended.

"Study wolves…. What do you want to know about wolves? Can't you just find that in a library or something?" Taylor questioned.

"Well," I paused a moment. "You're probably going to find this kind of silly, but I guess in a way, I've really come out here chasing folklore."

"Folklore? You're chasing the wolf that ate Grandma or something?" Taylor grunted twice in an attempt to laugh, but it seemed that his sides were starting to hurt him.

"The feathered wolf," I stated sternly.

"What the hell's a feathered wolf, like half-dog, half-bird?" Taylor's sarcasm wasn't offensive at all. It was

25

more humorous than anything, and I believe that's the way he meant it.

"You want to hear it? The story, that is?"

"Oh, I got to. A damn wolf with feathers. Who ever heard of such?" Taylor shook his head, smiling with disbelief. I'm sure he found humor with the odd image portrayed in his mind.

I leaned over into the back seat, plundering through my bags. "Here it is." I pulled a copy of the legend from my journal, sharing the story with Taylor as we continued to battle up the road. He was silent the entire time. After I finished reading the legend, I placed my journal back into my bag. Taylor continued to sit for a minute, without sound.

Taylor then cleared his throat. "You think that's real?" Confusion wrinkled his face.

"Who knows?" I responded, shrugging my shoulders. "If it's not, I've got nothing to lose. I need an animal to study for one of my classes anyway. I'm sure that I can find plenty of wildlife to document on Isle Royale, even if I don't see a wolf."

"John, I really hope that you do get to see a wolf. I don't know about one of these feathered ones, but to me a wolf's a wolf and I hope you don't get bitten. Lutsen, ten miles!" he shouted out. "Let me share some real stories with you, some law dog stories," Taylor growled. He and I both laughed periodically as the last ten miles of our journey together was filled with several short tales of heroism, chivalry, and a couple of nonsensical happenings. Even though I knew Taylor would always hate wolves, I only hoped that meeting me would change his view on killing them. Meeting him had definitely helped me to realize that every second of life is precious and should be enjoyed to the fullest, even if you're only blessed with the simplest of things.

Taylor dropped me off at a small gas station on highway sixty-one. "Just keep heading north," he pointed, "right up this road. I'm sure somebody will come along and carry you the rest of the way."

"How much farther is it?"

Taylor paused for thought. "About thirty, maybe forty miles."

After unloading my gear, I thanked Taylor for all of his help. If he had not intervened in Duluth, my life could have taken a very different path. For this, I was extremely grateful. I waved as he rattled away contently in Sweet Pea. I knew at that moment, in the years to come, I would remember Taylor and these memories would be good.

Chapter 3
ACHIEVEMENT

"Almost there," I thought to myself as I made tracks in the grass along the edge of the highway. As the distance between myself and Duluth lengthened, interaction with other humans began to fade away. I was entering into an almost unsettled world. Tall, magnificent conifers stood strong to my left, using their twisted roots to hold themselves erect. To my right were the seemingly endless waters of Lake Superior. Gulls and other winged fliers circled above the great blue engulfment in hopes of locating an easy meal. Squawks, calls, and warnings echoed all around me. An occasional dive into the water below would, each and every time, produce a frenzy over an unlucky trout or some other finned swimmer. These aerial daredevils would battle it out until one was finally able to choke the meal completely down. This would happen with almost every catch.

I walked all afternoon, sometimes holding my thumb out at the occasional passersby. By the evening, I was starting to get tired and hungry. I kept telling myself, one more mile and then I'll rest. But one more just wasn't enough. I pressed on into the darkness. The warm sunshine that caressed my back all day had been replaced by cool, moist air coming off the lake beside me. The sounds of the gulls and such that I had listened to earlier were being replaced by the squeals, croaks, and hoots of Superior's night creatures. An owl, who sounded not so far off, called to its mate in the distance. I listened quietly as they closed the gap between themselves, stopping only to vocalize their locations. A dim gray light shadowed the surface of the earth. I looked up to find a sliver of moon, rising ever so high. Instantly, I thought of wolves and wondered if I would get to hear one.

Around midnight, I decided to call it a day. I was able to bumble around in the darkness and find a small flat of ground just off the highway. There would be no tent for the night. I would just slumber in my sleeping bag, exposing myself to the millions of stars shining above. Sore and exhausted, I remember my last thoughts before dozing off, "It's a beautiful world and I'm thankful to be part of it." The chirping of locusts and black crickets softly sang me into a deep sleep. I slept for several hours, until Skipper arrived.

BOOM! A loud explosion echoed up the highway, waking me. "What the hell?" I said aloud, quickly sitting up. At first, I thought someone had shot at me. Just as that thought entered my mind, I heard the near-deafening sound again. Then, a ragged old pickup, pulling an even worse looking boat, rounded the curve in an all-out battle against gravity, friction, and every law of modern physics.

29

Driving junk seemed to be the going thing around here,
but being a motor-less vagrant myself, who was I to
judge? The old Ford, obviously exhausted, choked, spit,
and sputtered, finally giving up no more than ten feet
from my camp. I watched in amazement, half in, half out
of my bedding, as the iron beast fought for its last breath.
Chaclugg! Complete silence set in for a moment, a
moment that seemed to progress forward at half speed, as
I tried to wake.

The hair raised on the back of my neck as the driver's
window squealed its way down. An old, wrinkled hand
reached out to open the rusty door from the outside.
"Sorry to wake you, son."

As the door opened, I replied, "That's okay. It's about
time for me to get up anyway." It wasn't completely light
yet, but I supposed it was time to resume my traveling.

"I don't know what's wrong with this darn thing. It
seems every time I get on a little hill, she just starts
showing out." A small drawn-up old man, looking to be in
his eighties, energetically slid from the driver's seat. He
stormed his way to the front of the vehicle and attempted
to lift the hood.

"Hold on just a second, mister. I'll give you a hand." I
kicked out of my sleeping bag, then lifted the hood for the
old-timer.

He reached in probing, prodding, and pulling on
everything he could grab. "Stupid thing, I can't see
anything wrong." He grumbled a few more words, under
his breath, while scratching his balding head. Thick,
black-rimmed glasses covered his scaly blue eyes and

bushy brows.

"Mind if I take a look? I've worked on quite a few tractors back home," I yawned.

"Won't bother me; I don't see how you can hurt anything." Handing me his flashlight, he pulled on his suspenders in an attempt to adjust his sagging old jeans. He then snapped the two remaining buttons on his trashed-out raincoat. Through the scuffs and stains, some yellow still remained.

After a minute, I found the problem. "Your coil wire is shorting out on the frame." I pointed at the charred, deteriorated wire.

"Well, I'll be. Looks like those tractors back home paid off. What can we do with it?" he asked.

"Do you have any electrical tape?"

He thought for a second, then dove in behind the seat of his pickup. A can of Vienna sausages, several old receipts, one sock, and a half pack of gum came falling out onto the ground below. After giving up on the driver's side, he hurried to the passenger door, basically pulling out the same useless items. "No, no kind of tape at all."

I knew exactly what was in my packs, there was no use in digging through them. "Tell you what, give me that sock." I cut a short piece of twine that dangled from my backpack. After covering the damaged wire, I told the old timer to try it.

He gave me an unsure look at first, then replied, "If you think it'll work." As soon as he turned the key, the engine purred to life.

"Now, you know that's just temporary, right?"

"Sure, I do. As soon as I get back from the lake, I'll get her fixed. Get in. I know you don't want to stay here."

"No, I'm on my way to Grand Portage, then Isle Royale from there."

"Son, today is your lucky day. Skipper can take you all the way." The old man chuckled, obviously pleased with his poetics.

"Skipper, my name is John." I tossed my bags into the back of the pickup and we were on our way. "You can get me to Isle Royale?"

"Sure can. I was planning on trolling within a couple of miles of there. It won't hurt me to carry you on in."

"I've got reservations for a flight out tomorrow, then back Saturday."

"Have you already paid?"

"No, I haven't."

"Then what's the worry? What is it, probably a hundred, maybe one fifty, for that seaplane, right? I'll be fishing that same spot come Saturday."

I thought for a moment, then concluded that Skipper was right. I could be on the island today instead of tomorrow and save money. "Are you sure that's not going to put you in a bind?"

"Son, I troll these waters just about every day of the week. What else is a man my age going to do?"

I accepted the kind offer, "If it's not any trouble...." Skipper cut me off.

"None at all."

"Well, I guess you're right, Skipper, this does seem to be my lucky day."

"If you don't mind me asking, what makes you want to go that old Godforsaken chunk of rock anyway?"

I didn't want to argue wolves with Skipper this early in the morning, or really any other time. I've never met anyone from his era who wasn't hard stuck in their beliefs and would damn well die for them. "Wildlife. I'm doing a wildlife study for a zoology class back in New York."

"You came all the way up here from New York to look at some birds and stuff?" Skipper fought the slack in the steering while we both raised our voices above the loud shrill created by the cool morning air pushing through the leaky window seals.

"That and to get away from the city for a bit."

"I would have never thought you for a city boy."

"I'm not, just going to school there."

After chatting a bit more, we both settled back quietly. With conversation hindered by the high wind noise, it was much easier to just enjoy the ride without words. I peacefully watched as the sun continued to rise over the lake, bringing all forms of diurnal life with it. Once again, the gulls, loons, martins, and other birds of Superior resumed their daily activities. It seemed as though there was a magical shelf somewhere, where the glory of day and night could be changed out every twelve hours.

Just south of Grand Portage, Skipper wheeled us into a public boat launch. "We're done with the road," he stated. "Now, if we can get this old thing started, we'll be on the water. This will be the fun part. Have you ever been on a boat, John?"

"I sure have. When my dad was still alive, we'd go

33

out on Crow Creek almost every weekend in the summer. We'd stay for the whole weekend, sometimes." I jumped out of the truck to guide Skipper back onto the boat launch. This was really the first time I had taken a good look at The Princess King. "Shoddy and faded" would describe everything about her. Her hull was a common design from the 1960s, most of which had been retired or rotted away. Her wooden planks looked as though any day could be the last and the walk-through windshield would definitely have to be peered over; transparency had long left these fitted protectors. The seats were badly torn and various items lay freely on the floor, waiting to ramble about. Trimmed out with gold spray paint, I only hoped that she would float. Luckily, she did. Within no time, we were being pushed across the lake by a ragged, off-white Johnson outboard.

Skipper grinned, looking at me. "See? I told you this was the fun part." It was evident that Skipper truly loved the water. He had said nothing about family, friends, or even home, for that matter.

I was curious, "Skipper, what does your wife think about you spending so much time on the water?"

"No wife," he responded. "No wife, no kids, no worries."

"You've never been married at all, Skipper?" I hoped I wasn't prying too far, but, again, I was curious.

"No.... There was one that I fell head over heels for when I was in my early twenties. She broke my heart, twisted me up, and threw me away." He then said, slowly with a sigh, as though his thoughts were a million miles away, "Norma Jean Sanders."

"That bad, huh?" I was sympathetic, but still curious.

"Yeah, we courted for two years. I asked her to marry me, and she said yes. I bought a ring and even found us a place to live. Then some cowboy from Wyoming came through with the rodeo. She fancied him, and there was nothing I could do. I guess me being a store clerk wasn't nearly as exciting as a man on a bull. I haven't been to another rodeo since."

"What about dating? Did you date anyone after?"

"Well, there were a couple of girls, nothing serious. How about you, John, do you have a girlfriend or a wife?"

"No wife. I haven't had any girlfriends lately either. It's been kinda hard for me to find my place in the Big Apple."

"That's where you're going to school, right?"

I nodded. "I'm from South Carolina, though. I had a few girlfriends back there. I guess they liked rodeo men too…. I'm sorry, Skipper; I shouldn't have said that."

"Oh, don't be sorry, son. You wasn't even thought about when that happened. You're a rodeo man, John?" Skipper held the helm steady, as The Princess King continued to growl toward the unseen island.

"I rode a few bulls as a teenager, never traveled with it, though. How long have you had this old boat, Skipper?" I could tell that talking about Norma Jean was depressing the old fisherman and we needed to change the subject. I didn't really care about the shoddy, old boat, or how many years she had been on this earth, just as long as she kept us afloat.

35

"About twenty years." He thought a second, "Maybe twenty-two." A light chop was starting on the water. It had been really smooth up to this point, allowing us to cruise around seven or eight knots. Skipper eased off the throttle, slowing us just a bit. "It won't be long now." He pointed in the distance. Through the haze, the island was coming into view while dark purple clouds were starting to build in the east.

"How far, Skipper, do you think that is?" I felt compelled to keep conversation going; talk that didn't pertain to past relationships, that is.

Skipper squinted, "probably five miles or so. On a good clear day, you can see twice that far."

Small rolling waves were forming as far as the eye could see. Rhythmic slaps from the water could be heard as they bounced and spattered off the wooden hull. I was starting to fail in my goal to keep conversation going. The sight of Isle Royale had me mesmerized. The reality of possibly completing my journey was setting in on me. It made me nervous, excited, and somewhat afraid all at the same time.

Only the low growl of the boat motor and the consistent slap of the waves could be heard as we closed the distance between us and the island. The tall balsam firs, coming into view, made the whole place look like a tribute to the Christmas holidays. I could only imagine how beautiful a light snow held in their dark green branches would be. Rocky shores separated the large land mass from the waters of the lake. Jagged and disrupted, they showed no sign of consistency. At about fifty yards out, I was able to see movement along the heavy trunk of a tall jack pine. Its hefty brown bark resembled thousands of thick, muddy footprints left by small children. Its branches carried needles instead of leaves, much like the Balsam Firs, only not as thick. Getting closer, the moving images began to fill in with color and outline, presenting three large red squirrels scurrying along the timbers. Continuing forward, their razor-sharp claws became audible as they ripped along from tree to tree. They fussed and clamored about, climbing high into the safety of their natural world, hiding themselves from the strange newcomers aboard The Princess King.

Skipper pulled back on the throttle, completely killing the engine. "Well son, here we are—Isle Royale."

"My God, it's beautiful," I responded, never looking back at Skipper. Isle Royale did not resemble any island I had ever seen. It looked more like its own country. "This is what a one hundred thirty thousand acre wilderness looks like… amazing, completely amazing." I could hardly believe my own eyes. Isle Royale was enormous, being forty-five miles long and roughly nine miles wide.

"We better hurry and get you unloaded. That storm is coming this way and it's getting stronger." Skipper pulled his hat down on his head to keep the wind from taking it.

I had been completely taken by the island, ignoring the storm that was steadily building around us. The rocking of the boat, loud slaps against the hull, and growing swells had eluded my attention for the latter part of the trip. "I'm sorry, Skipper. I kind of lost myself for a few minutes there." I tossed my bags onto the shore, then jumped for a rocky crest no more than three feet from the bow. Turning back, I smiled with heart-felt satisfaction, "Thanks Skipper, I really appreciate this."

"No time for hugs and kisses, now. You need to get yourself some shelter and I need to get back to the mainland." The storm and visibility were both growing worse by second. "I'll see you Saturday around noon." Skipper waved goodbye, slipping The Princess King into reverse.

Watching the fog swallow him up, I hoped Skipper wouldn't have too much trouble finding his way back. I gathered my belongings and made way for higher ground. Looking back one last time, I could see the waves had almost doubled in height. I was concerned about Skipper, but he was an experienced seaman and had probably seen much worse. Quickly throwing a tarp over myself and my equipment, I held the corners tight while the wind roared around me. Even though a violent storm was tearing away at the island, a feeling of warmth came over me. I was happy to be where I was. The first half of my journey was no longer a goal, but an achievement.

With a loud thunderclap, the spirit of the wolf screamed out, penetrating my soul. This was the first time that I'd been awake for one of the callings. It was louder than ever before and resembled the scream of a hawk, but I knew it belonged to the ghost of gray. I knew it belonged to the one who had been haunting me. It belonged to the wolf, and I was now on his ground. I had finally broken the bourne.

Chapter 4
MAKING CAMP

The storm receded after several hours of fury, but thankfully I had managed to keep myself and my equipment mostly dry. Peeling back the tarp that had been my roof and walls for several hours, the calm, quiet, and tranquil surroundings eased in. For a few minutes I lay still, watching the small upward lift of spring leaves each time a drop of water would slide from the waxy topsides. Under some trees, puddles would catch these drops, disrupting the small pools with quickly expanding ripples. The widening rings would fade, seemingly at the same rate they came about. Slowly, the birds inhabiting the island came back to life, singing goodbye to the rains and hello to the many worms and insects that the downpour had pushed up from the soil. I stood tall, stretching, to make myself right again after being in a ball for so long. Full-blown spring was on the horizon. Some evidence of winter was still around with many leafless trees, but just as many were starting to fill their branches with new life.

Despite the desire to just run through the wilderness,

hoping to trip over a wolf, I took the time to update my journal. Up to this point, I had recorded every event to the fullest description possible even though I knew most would not pertain in the least to my final essay. My journal was my log, my record of the entire expedition, and I did not want to cheat myself with lack of information in the end.

After completing the entry of the day's events, I read back to the night I shared with Candance. "What a woman," I shook my head, smiling, then put my journal back into its original place of transport and hung my camera around my neck. I was ready to start exploring. Throwing my survival pack over my back, I left everything else with the intention of finding a more desirable campsite later.

April/6/89 2:00pm

--Today will always seem like D-day to me, as I consider myself deployed. The journey to Isle Royale is behind me. Now begins the search for an exceptionally elusive creature and the struggle (or should I say the much-appreciated opportunity) of living primitively.

April/6/89 7:00pm

--This morning, after the rainstorm, I ventured about two miles from my original landing. The forest here is dense and populated with many varieties of tall, strong trees. The sounds of wildlife echo throughout. No wolf

*signs were discovered today. I will set up camp tonight
and search again tomorrow.*

After building a campfire, more for light than heat, I
erected my small tent and began to situate everything in
its place of order. The site I chose was no more than thirty
feet inland from my drop point. Earlier, I had decided that
there was no use in dragging all of my gear halfway
across the island just to have to bring it all back again in a
few days. The reason for moving camp any at all was for
fear, that if by chance a boater happened by while I was
gone, he would not have such easy pickings. I found the
sound of the fire, popping and crackling, very relaxing.
Lying back on a grassy spot, at the edge of the burning
branches, I was getting the solitude I so much needed.
After a helping of beef jerky and canned peas, I retired for
the evening. An early start was what I wanted for the next
morning.

After placing my journal in a pocket under the mesh
window, I turned off the small light that dangled from the
peak of my tent. Wolves, not relaxation, were my reason
for being here, and there would be no staying up late or
sleeping in.

Early the next morning I stoked the coals left from the
night before, creating a small radiant glow. The morning
was cool, cool enough to warrant a thin jacket and thick
socks. Squatting over the edge, I tried to soak up some
heat from the embers then poured straight coffee, just
after the kettle whistled.

April/7/89 5:30 a.m.

--I am wide awake and have been awake for about an hour. I think possibly the howling of a wolf might have woken me, but I'm not sure. It is cold, probably around forty degrees Fahrenheit. After coffee and sunup, I will continue my search.

Sounds of life began to crowd the shores as the dark morning was slowly replaced by the coming light. Birds, squirrels, even geese could be heard scurrying, squawking, and honking about. I strained for the blood-chilling howl I wanted to hear so badly, but none entertained my awaiting ear. I wondered for a moment, as I sipped my hot morning brew, if I had made a mistake pursuing such a foolish thing. Then I heard my father's voice, "Press on, son, press on."

Press on I did. After extinguishing the hint of a campfire, I packed two days' rations, a compass, and a solar blanket. I planned on coming back to camp but thought it wise to prepare for the worst. As I started to leave camp, I thought about my journal. I knew if I left it, something would happen to it. I needed my journal as much as my camp gear. Without it, I would have to try and remember every detail of the trip. I wanted my documents to be precise. I decided then that my journal would not leave my side from here out.

Fifty yards or so from camp, I picked up on a small animal trail that I had not seen the afternoon before. The trail was well defined and seemed to be leading into the heart of the island. I followed along slowly, watching and searching for any sign that might indicate wolves, but I would have no luck. Tracks would not be present on such a rocky floor. I could only hope that there would be sandy spots along the way. Wild ferns, two to three feet in height, were scattered all throughout as far as the forest would allow me to see. The terrain was far from flat, but hilly with many crests and outcroppings of large stones and winter-drained grasses. All green and moisture seemed to have been sucked out of each blade, leaving them to a light beige color. Deepening into the island, the balsam firs were progressively replaced with paper and yellow birch and what seemed to be some type of poplar. The balsam firs were still present, just not as dominant as they were along the shoreline. Unlike the fir, the birch and poplar carried leaves on their branches instead of needles. But all seemed to belong exactly where they had been placed, making the entire island wild and beautiful throughout.

Several times along the way, I would quickly stop after hearing brush rustle or a limb break. Sometimes the culprit would show face, but not always. Usually, the sounds were the results of the (*Tamiasciurus hudsonicus*) red squirrel. I looked at my watch. I had been hiking for almost three hours on very rough terrain. Ahead was a boulder that overlooked a small valley. It looked to be a great place to rest.

April/7/89   8:45am

--I've been walking in the forest for nearly three hours. No signs of wolves inhabiting the area yet. (Tamiasciurus hudsonicus) The red squirrel is abundant and very energetic.

After sitting on the large rock and reading over the journal entry I'd just made, it became clear to me that detailed documentation of the red squirrels might be necessary for my class project. If I did not find the creature I was looking for, at least I would have something to fall back on. Quenching my thirst with water from my canteen, my journey resumed.

My walk continued to be slow, and my attention was set on even the smallest of details. By this point I had crossed many sandy areas, but no tracks were found. No tracks of any animal, thanks to the torrential downpour from the day before. Even without discovering any wolf signs, I was completely content to be a visitor in such a wonderful place. I thought about the research I had done before leaving the city and how it would be useful in helping me find Green Stone Ridge tomorrow. I hoped finding the ridge and trekking along the crest would prove more productive by having the help of a constantly elevated view. I also wanted to see the greenish basalt outcroppings I had read about.

Around two in the afternoon, I decided to start making a gradual turn to the south. My trek had been mostly to the east up until this point. I made a gradual turn southward then set my sights due west. By my calculations, this would put me back at camp before sundown.

April/7/89 6:45 p.m.

*--Today my search for wolves proved unproductive. I
am enjoying the solitude and peace the undisturbed
wilderness has to offer. My search has been slow and
cautious, only covering about six miles. Tomorrow, I will
begin to document the red squirrel as back-up.*

After updating my journal, I rolled an old stump into
camp that I'd passed on the trail a short way back. It was
not the most comfortable of stools, but at least it gave me
the option of sitting somewhere other than on the damp
ground. Removing my hat, I ran my hands through my
oily hair, then caressed the splotchy stubble that had been
pushing out on my face since Duluth. Laughing with a
short inner grunt, I knew that I must be looking a little
rough. But here, appearance didn't matter, and I was glad
of that.

Gathering up several fallen branches, I set them
ablaze as night fell. After putting a large can of vegetable
beef soup at the edge of the coals, I sat slumped over with
my elbows on my knees on the makeshift stool and started
singing the only lines I could remember to a song my
mom had written years back. Deepening my voice and
adding as much country twang as possible, I belted out,
"He got a John Deere tractor with no field to plow, gonna
buy him some land someday, somehow. Got a fifty-seven
Chevy sittin' up on blocks, it won't run but she sho'

means a lot." This continued for over an hour, progressively quieting as the night grew later, pausing occasionally for a bite of soup.

Suddenly, my off-key entertainment was brought to an abrupt halt by the explosive howl of an Eastern timber wolf. Almost in disbelief, I immediately stopped singing and ceased all movement. I felt unsure of the sound that I thought I had heard. I know that sometimes when someone wants to hear something so badly, his mind can transform a like sound into an audible bringing of what he might want to hear. After sitting utterly motionless for a minute or two, I decided to distance myself from the crackling fire. If I could be blessed with such an acoustical event once more, I wanted a totally undisturbed environment. I crept away from camp on my tiptoes. Standing as a statue at the edge of darkness, the piercing sound burst through the night once again. This was definitely no figment of my imagination. It was, this time, without dispute, the cry of the gray ghost. The voice of the wolf had oppressed all other sounds, declaring itself as king of the night.

The hair on the back of my neck stood erect as I witnessed a third calling. Far, far in the distance, the cry was answered. Possibly a sibling, possibly a parent, or maybe an enemy from a neighboring pack, this I could only assume. I stood listening for quite some time after the last call. A ringing in my ears became nearly deafening as I strained for one more sound from the wolves. It never came.

April/7/89 9:45 p.m.

--I did not finish dinner tonight as I lost interest in eating after hearing, for the first time, the blood chilling cry of an Eastern timber wolf. Canis lupus lycaon, until now proved to be very elusive; audibly and optically, avoiding any detection. On this night, I have witnessed three calls from the hidden carnivores.

Encouraged, hopeful, and heartened, all of these feelings brewed strongly within me. A sound never in my life meant as much to me as the voices I heard that night. It was a promise that maybe, just maybe, I, John Ryder, would have the rare opportunity to observe these magnificent creatures in their own free world. It was a glimpse of optimism that had been discouraged since the layover in New York. The search for Green Stone Ridge would be postponed. My direction tomorrow would be north. North, toward the voices that commanded me to do so.

April/8/89 6:00 a.m.

--Very little sleep last night after hearing the calls. Saturday is tomorrow. I am still worried that squirrels may have to become a priority in study. I continue to hear the voices in my sleep.

I tossed and turned all night. Every time I would start to doze off, a sound, any sound, would quickly bring me to my feet. My personal release of intestinal gases even woke me once, imitating the growl of an angry wolf in my own captive mind. I had to find these animals.

I left camp with my sleeping bag and a small amount of food. I knew that I needed to take complete advantage of this outing considering that the reunion with Skipper was at noon tomorrow. I trekked due north from camp for about half a mile, hastily, then slowed my pace and began looking for wolf signs. Judging from the sounds I had heard the night before, and considering the muffling of such a dense vegetation, I estimated the first wolf to have been in this area.

My observations were detailed and precise. I tried to keep my movements quiet and concealed as much as possible, but also quick. This continued throughout the entire morning. Around noon, I was beginning to tire and becoming discouraged. My efforts had proven fruitless.

April/8/89 12:35 p.m.

--At this point I am very disappointed. I have not been able to locate any sign of last night's callers. If things continue in this manner, I will be forced to observe tree rats starting this afternoon.

After resting a bit, I loaded my gear onto my back and resumed the search. I continually tried to dampen each and every step while progressing through thick underbrush. Occasionally, I would find small animal trails that would help in doing this. Around four in the afternoon, I came upon a large bog located approximately three miles from camp. I spent hours among the black spruce, searching the soft earth for evidence of the wolf's existence. It was hopeless. All my efforts seemed to be in vain.

April/8/89 6:35 p.m.

--I am sitting in an opening of approximately three acres on the edge of a large bog. Several red squirrel nests are in the area, and I am starting to see movements in the distant treetops. As with other squirrels, dusk seems to motivate their return to these large nests, which rest mostly in the tops of hardwood trees. These animals are very large in size and numbers. They are mostly red in color, but some are a dark shade of brown.

Just as I was about to jot down more information on the red squirrels, I heard a loud crash coming from the woods to the right of the clearing.

Focusing my attention in that direction, I sat motionless, letting nothing move except for my eyes. The crashing continued, sounding as if whatever heavy-bodied animal was making the noise was on a direct path toward the opening. Suddenly, the brush along the edge shook violently and a large bull moose bolted from the thicket, trotting directly into the clearing. He stopped about the middle then raised his head high, loudly taking in the air around him. A thick mucus spewed from his nostrils as he exhaled. Antlers like crude, prickly boat paddles adorned his large head. The massive animal must have stood six feet high. After checking for scents that might be lying on the wind, he continued his direction of travel, exiting the clearing just as abruptly as he had entered.

"Something spooked him," I said almost silently, looking back in the direction he first came from. No sooner than I looked, a smaller-bodied creature darted back and forth, partially hidden by the thick underbrush and partly obscured by the fading evening light. Then, a small red fox shot into the clearing, bringing his body into full view. A limp deer mouse dangled from his mouth, just before being tossed playfully about. The fox ran a few circles around his meal then crouched in the grass, ready to pounce again. This continued for several minutes until an unrestrained cough from my own self sent the animal running quickly for cover; so quickly, he left his tormented treat to do the same but in a much more crippled state.

April/8/89 7:15 p.m.

--This venture proved to be more dramatic than any other outing so far. I witnessed a very large bull-moose leave the safety of thick cover, exposing itself in full view. This revelation was encouraged by the playful actions of a small red fox as he tossed a deer mouse about. Unfortunately, I startled the fox, or I may have been entertained for a much longer period than I was.

I continued to sit silent until the coming of darkness

50

inevitably obscured all visual continuity between myself and the clearing below. After unrolling my sleep sack, I laid down in the same location as where I had sat while witnessing the earlier events. I felt fortunate on one hand but lacking on the other. I was glad to have been a spectator of such natural wonders, but still, the wolves had eluded me. The wolves were where my heart was. Without them, this heart that felt warmed by the sighting of the moose and the fox, also felt empty. Tomorrow this heart would have to return to the modern world, unfulfilled.

Chapter 5
WAITING REUNION

Leaving the clearing beside the bog at first light, my movements were hasty and my steps quick. I stopped only to untangle myself from a heavy mess of fishing line that had found its way onto the island. My mind was far from content and my heart even farther. I had spent all this time and effort for nothing more than squirrels. The thought of returning to Carter's class with documented activities of rodents sickened me. My research would be equivalent to that of students who had spent, at most, an hour in Central Park. The short encounter with the fox and the moose would make good attributes, but they would not credit enough time for a subject studied.

"Damn!"

I broke camp and was waiting at the pickup point by eleven a.m. I sat silent, nearly thoughtless, awaiting Skipper's arrival. Staring into the distance for one, two, then three hours, I saw nothing but a great liquid engulfment with an endless, flat surface. In my boredom, I tossed small pebbles into the water just inches in front of me. Nearly mesmerized by the tiny circular patterns, I waited patiently, convinced that at any moment The Princess King would break the horizon. Hours went by until the sun itself became the only object to touch this never-ending union of above and below.

"I know he didn't forget." I began talking to myself, reassuring myself, trying to find reason for Skipper's tardiness. "He didn't seem to have Alzheimer's." Tossing another pebble into the water below, I watched as the ripples slowly dissipated. They reminded me of the surging waves that Skipper and I weathered together. "The storm!" The thought of Skipper sinking during the storm flashed through my mind. It was as realistic as me being stranded on this desolate island. "My God." I cupped my hands and placed them over my face, muffling my words. "Surely not. Boat trouble... Yeah, I bet that's it." I laughed, "The Princess King has let us down." I was almost positive that Skipper had had boat trouble or even problems with his old pickup and would be on as soon as possible. I built a small fire and bedded down at the pickup point, feeling certain that the old mariner would show by morning.

"Woooooolf..." A strong whispering voice broke through the darkness, silencing all others. The night fog that had settled in around me parted with the enchanted one's whisper, bringing with it an eerie chill but at the same time, conflicting warmth. I was awake when I first heard the call, but soon fell asleep only to hear more. Over and over the spirit haunted my dreams until I was awakened.

April/9/89 11:45 p.m.

--Wolves have awakened me. It sounds as though they are hunting something. Many calls have been made and seem to be coming from five to ten different animals. It is hard to tell exactly how many there actually are because they are in pursuit of something, and their positions are changing rapidly.

The chase went on for about an hour, keeping my utmost attention. Not for one moment during this did I think about Skipper or the possibility of being stranded on this remote land mass. It sounded like the hunt ended within a mile east of my camp. It was close enough that once the animal was taken down, I could hear the alpha's warning to the other members of the pack to stay clear as they ripped the favored intestines from the still warm body. I finally lay down a couple of hours after midnight, once all was quiet.

April/10/89 5:40 a.m.

--No sign of Skipper so far. I had very little sleep last night due to the chase. I listened to the pack feed on what I assume to be a moose until two in the morning.

I made a small fire close to the edge of the water, then dug the kettle and some coffee from my pack. After watching the sun come up in the east, my focus was turned to the west, awaiting the arrival of The Princess

King. Graphic images of last night's kill crept into my mind. I could not help but to think that a moose caught up in the complete cycle of life might prove to be a sufficient study. Tossing more small pebbles into the water, I tried to remember the chase, sound by sound. I could clearly imagine each action taking place. Mentally, I tried to match every howl, every growl, and every cry, each with its own personal identity. In my mind, there were wolves on every hillside, patiently pushing their distance closer and closer, finally encompassing their prey after a well-organized strategy of entrapment. All communicated in a language only they could truly understand, and used that same language to force the unfortunate one to make quick and nervous decisions and eventually, inevitably, the attack. The alphas initiated the bloody engagement, hanging from the rear, using their weight to bring the animal down. It began to sway, losing its footing. The others jumped in, pressing their jowls around its vulnerable neck. Almost instantly, the pressure was too much, puncturing the vessels and the airway, sending the adrenaline-filled blood rushing into his lungs. With only seconds to live, he struggled, bellowing out for someone, anyone, to help, spraying a mist of crimson red into the air. This only excited the predators even more. Finally, after all the struggle, he laid his head over to die and the wolves began to feed. With his last moments of cognition, his eyes rolled back then glassed over. Death overcame him. He was finally free.

"I gotta see, I gotta go see." To see and study these mystical creatures was rapidly becoming more important to me than anything else, even leaving the island.

I grabbed my camera, along with my journal, then ran as fast as I could toward what I imagined to be a broken, mutilated body that I somehow hoped to find. I was lucky. It was as if my senses led me straight to it. I could smell the death quite some distance away. It's understandable to smell old death, as the vultures do. I had done that before, but this was new death. New, as in less than eight hours from being a beating heart with a working, functional frame and a spirit that desired to live, reproduce, and be an intricate part of such a beautiful and majestic place. I guess, even dead, this moose was being just that. He was part of the cycle that allowed a place such as this to exist. I stopped on a small hill, overlooking the corpse. It was a moose and the white of his skeleton glistened in the morning sun.

But, as I started to approach, something else caught my attention. Something was struggling in the thick to the left of me. I could see an image through the dense underbrush, jumping, pulling, and tussling about, but not really going anywhere. I quietly crept toward the commotion.

Cautiously making my way through the brush, I could finally see. It was a wolf. A beautiful, Eastern timber wolf; grey with markings of black. Her piercing eyes burned into mine as she peered from behind a tall hardwood. They were like diamonds with hundreds of segmented lines the color of a flaming moon. She could neither run nor attack. She was entangled in the same piece of fishing line that had snared me the day before.

We stared into each other's non-blinking souls for what seemed to be an unbroken stretch of eternity. She showed absolutely no fear with her tail high, sharp pointed ears turned back, and her long glistening teeth exposed. She was ready for engagement of the worst. Watching her stand so strong, all alone, I instantly thought her to be the alpha female of her pack.

Slowly, at a short distance, I sat on the bare ground in open view. Her aggressive behavior toward me continued for hours. I began to periodically look away in hopes of showing some subordinance. She never took her eyes off me. By these actions, I knew her to be the dominant of the females. I continued to wait patiently.

"Skipper," I whispered softly. I thought about the chase last night and all that I heard. It became obvious to me that when The Princess King decided to make her way to the island, it would be with no less noise than the wolves made during the chase. I should be able to hear The Princess King from my current location and would be able to make my way to the pickup point in just a matter of minutes.

Turning my attention back to the wolf, we continued our near motionless greeting. Reasons for Skipper's tardiness began to develop in my mind. Maybe it was an act of God. It was an act that would not only allow me to save the life of this trapped animal, but it would also give me what I needed to carry back for my study. I felt sure that this beautiful creature would allow me to free her and as soon as I did, the loud buzz of Skipper's old outboard would be heard. With these thoughts of false confidence, I

57

snapped a few pictures of the captive animal, then raised myself from my submissive position and stepped forward. At the same time, she lunged, nearly deafening me with the loud aggression of an attempted attack. I did not think about the line stretching, but if I had made my safe distance an inch closer, I would have lost my face.

"Shit!!!" I scrambled back quickly, shouting aloud, "Wolves are wild, stupid!" I could not believe that I had allowed myself to be foolish enough to think otherwise. Clearly, this building of trust would take longer than I wanted. I hoped that Skipper would be perfectly late. If I missed a couple of days of school, that would be fine. I was truly where I wanted to be.

We continued to sit silently while a bright moon pushed its way upward. Eventually, the idea of being completely motionless had simply become an idea. Hungry mosquitoes were starting to rise up from their winter slumber, showing that spring was finally here. I tried to move slowly to mash the tiny vampires, which the wolf seemed to tolerate, but it just wasn't enough. Not long after dark, the constant attack from thousands, maybe millions, of the tiny bloodsuckers had taken a toll on me. I could fight them no longer. I would have to retreat to camp, dousing what was left of my punctured body with repellant, taking refuge within the walls of my tent.

April/10/89 10:32pm

--After hours of wandering, I have finally found my

way back to camp. Earlier today, I ventured to last night's kill site. I was right, it was a moose, a bull at that. But even more, the alpha female of a wolf pack is still there, tangled in heavy fishing line. I have tried to gain her trust so that she will allow me to free her, but this will take some time. Considering the difficulty in finding my way back to camp in the dark, I will wait until first light to return.

As soon as the sky turned pink, I was on my way. No fire, no coffee, no Skipper, and honestly no interest in any of these. I believe that if I had heard The Princess King, I would have just ignored her.

Once close to the site, I slowed my pace so as not to spook the wolf. Upon approach, I saw her still body lying on the leafless ground. Then I saw something that frightened me so badly my whole body seized up: blood, and a lot of it. Not moose blood: her blood, fresh and large in quantity, spilled all around her, mashed into the soil and matted into her fur. I approached her cautiously, gently nudging her with a stick from nearby. She seemed lifeless, and nearly dead. A wire leader, attached to the fishing line had ripped her inner thigh completely open. I wanted to panic, but I knew that wouldn't save her.

Cutting the fishing line from her limp body, I gathered her up into my arms and started back to camp. Using my shirt to hold pressure on the wound, the liquid of life still slowly seeped from her. I walked gently, but as swiftly as possible, careful not to cause her any more pain than necessary. I'm sure, if there had been any people around, we would have been a frightening sight as we approached the edge of the island. Laying her down softly, the wound was gently dressed. The bandages, made from my t-shirt, quickly deepened from white to red. She was going to die, and it was killing me that I could not save her. "Mud!" I thought about mud. "That'll stop the bleeding." Quickly running to the water's edge, I grabbed two fists full of mud then packed the wound. "That's the best I can do for you girl…. I really hope it works." Deep sorrow overpowered my heart.

Not taking my eyes off her all day, she remained motionless except for the faint up/down movement of her torso with each shallow breath. There was no sleep for me the first two nights that I had her. On the third, exhaustion overpowered me before the sun went down. I slept hard, hearing no voices, having no dreams, but my soul told me that something was watching… something very, very, different from anything I'd ever known.
April/14/89 7:00am

--I've neglected my journal for days. I have the wolf with me and have reestablished camp near the water's edge. The wolf was nearly dead when I found her, but now seems stable. This morning, I will look for freshwater mussels at the shoreline. I feel that a soup would be good for both of us, as my food supply is getting dangerously low. I have given her the Hebrew name Aniah, which means, "God has answered". Maybe later I will heat some water and try to clean the dried blood from her fur.

I left Aniah at camp, sleeping. Her breathing had progressively gotten stronger, and this eased my mind about leaving her alone. I hoped that I could find enough mussels along the shoreline without getting too far from her. I did not want to be gone for too long. Methodically, I made my way through ankle deep water, feeling with my bare feet for the tiny shell-bound creatures. Luckily, they were bountiful.

Ahead in the distance, I could see a wrecked vessel that had washed up on the bank. Black and blue shells were all around it. As I got closer, I could see that these creatures were gathered around the front half of an old boat with gold trim. It quickly became evident that they were sheltering around The Princess King. I stood mesmerized for quite some time.

"The storm." Standing alone on the rocky beach, tears filled my eyes. "I'm so sorry, Skipper," I whispered. "I am so, so sorry." I could not save him, but Aniah still had a chance.

Looking through the battered hull, I scavenged a short length of bow line. Skipper was gone and there was nothing I could do about that. I could stay here and mourn or make the best of my situation.

"Only, Aniah." I thought about Aniah. She needed me now. I could do nothing for Skipper except know that he lived a long life and died doing what he loved. Sadly, I made my way back to camp.

"Aniah, what will happen to us now?" I stroked her gently while we lay together on the soft bed of leaves that I had made for her. Once again, tears filled my eyes. I cried for Aniah. I cried for Skipper. And I cried for myself. I lay and wept for quite some time, crying in fear of what might happen next. I knew, somehow, I had to get off the island. But I also knew that I could not leave Aniah, not any time soon.

April/17/89 8:15pm

-- I've been nursing Aniah by day and signaling for help with large fires by night. I have made an S.O.S. on the shore with logs. Thankfully, Aniah is growing stronger. She is keeping her eyes open for hours at the time and has attempted to stand, but is still too weak. She has finally accepted me as her friend. I don't know if this relationship will continue once she is well enough to return to her pack, but I pray that it does. I pray even harder that she is able to return before I, myself, have to. I do not think I would be able leave her until she is truly ready.

Aniah grew stronger and stronger as the days went by. I became greatly concerned that when she regained enough strength, she might turn on me. However, it was quite the opposite. Our relationship grew with her recovery. Aniah proved to be beautiful inside and out. But I knew, soon, staying with a human would not be enough for her. She was the dominate female of her clan. She led the hunts, initiated the attacks, and had her choice of the kill. Much like Candance, the airline stewardess I had met, Aniah was very passionate. To lock her away inside of my confines would certainly drain the life from her, the very life I'd worked so hard to save. It was inevitable that soon she would have to walk out of my life and back into hers. I only hoped that she would wait until she was strong enough to regain her position as the alpha female and not find death trying. For two weeks, we ate freshwater mussels and wild blueberries. I was completely out of the food that I brought with me. I really needed to spend some time seeking out other sources.

"Tonight is the last night for mussels, Aniah." I spoke softly as I stirred what I hoped to be our last dish of these tiny aquatic creatures, for a while at least. "Tomorrow, I plan to set some snares for squirrels, and I'd like to see if we can get enough boards out of The Princess King to build a fish trap." Aniah looked at me deeply. At times, I swear, I think she knew everything I was saying. "Yep, I think if I take some of that fishing line—"

I was immediately quieted by a stern growl coming from deep within Aniah. Her piercing eyes were fixed on something hidden in the darkness behind me. Her warning steadily grew in volume and magnitude, telling whatever was brave enough to approach to get ready for hell. She stood high, back hair erect, teeth showing, and tail straight. I turned slowly, trying to make out the approaching adversary. It took a moment for my eyes to adjust to the darkness.

"My God," I whispered. Standing less than five feet from me was the biggest and blackest male wolf I had ever seen. He was as black as a demon and crept through the darkness, just the same. As I stared at him with complete fear, he took two small steps toward me that did not, in any way, let his presence be known. His movements were completely inaudible. He was obviously a born killer and perfect in his trade. The hair around his muzzle was red with blood from a kill. It looked as though it were still fresh. His eyes, fixed on mine, burned like the ball of fire our planet circles every day. Aniah continued to growl, deep from within herself, while he kept full attention on the island's intruder. I only hoped that he would not attack either of us. With his large size, I felt it would take him mere seconds to end my life and Aniah's too. Just as I thought I was about to lose all ability to breathe, think, or control any other function, the huge male wolf laid down. He lay down, submissively, on his stomach and began to inch his way toward Aniah. I could not believe that I was witnessing this giant male wolf submit to Aniah. I was almost sure that he was the alpha male when I first saw him, but now I didn't know what to think.

Motionless, I sat witnessing the reunion of these two magnificent animals. Aniah stopped threatening the intruder as soon as he turned his attention from me to her. They both began to whimper softly and lick each other's faces. They were very excited to see one another. As I watched Aniah lap the blood from the face of the male wolf, I remembered reading about how these creatures were sometimes considered more social than humans themselves. If this were true, I could only imagine how it must have felt to have had to leave her behind in that tangled mess of fishing line.

I spoke almost silently, still watching the affectionate display. "He is the alpha male. He's Aniah's mate." Together, they had built a family; a family that was nearly torn apart by her close encounter with death. I felt I would lose her that night.

No sooner had I thought about Aniah leaving than she did. She stopped in front of me and stared for a moment while her mate nudged her gently, encouraging her to run away with him. Her stare was not evil or intimidating in any way. It was a look of appreciation. A thank you for all that I had done. Then, as quickly as either had come into my life, they bounded away, disappearing into the darkness. She was once again a wolf, wild and free.

As for me, I was once again alone; a student with one blown semester but one hell of an experience. I was currently stranded on a huge wilderness island that might not underlie the foot of another human being for quite some time. I had done everything I knew to signal for help and thus far none of it had worked. But, to be honest, I was glad that it hadn't. Without my help, Aniah would have certainly perished.

Night after night, I added more and more wood to my fires, but still no help came. I was beginning to get discouraged and even though I was one of the world's biggest loners, I was starting to get downright lonely. That is, until Aniah came back.

Showing the same level of stealth the black male had, Aniah crept into my camp undetected. I was forcing myself to eat mussels and blueberries when I felt a haunting force penetrate through me. Looking up from my unwanted dish, I found her standing within arm's length, directly in front of me. "Aniah! You came back. Are you okay?" I asked earnestly, as though she could answer.

She answered, responding in her own way. Aniah slowly walked to me, laying her head in my lap. As soon as I started to pet her, she became as frisky as a small pup. She turned her head back and forth, gnawing at my hand, whining and whimpering with her tail wagging. I knew better, but it was as though she had become completely domesticated in the short time that we had spent together. Aniah was still a wolf at the peak of her life, and to be honest, I was a man at a very strange part of mine. But deep in me, I was beginning to feel that life here, with the wolf, was where I was meant to be. Aniah made me feel that way. I had helped her and now she was helping me. She stayed through the night as the guest of honor, eating every mussel I had gathered the morning before. We settled in for sleep around midnight, a man and his wolf.

The next morning, I awoke to find her gone. "Aniah!" I called out, pulling my jeans on. "Aniah, where are you girl?"

Stepping out of the tent, I looked down to find a much-appreciated gift left by Aniah. "Well, I'll be. I guess she knew I was getting sick and tired of eating those snotty little mussels." In the doorway, at my feet, was the first mink I had ever seen that some rich lady didn't have draped around her neck. For someone of royalty, this animal might have been worn to the Queen's Ball. For John Ryder, this long over-grown rat-like specimen would be breakfast and the smooth dark hide possibly a new cover for my journal.

May/1/89 10:05 am

--I had mink for breakfast this morning. It is possibly the best meal I've ever had, certainly beating the hell out of freshwater mussels and wild blueberries. It was a gift left by Aniah. I hope she will visit again soon. I also hope that she will bring more treats, as my traps, thus far, have proven to be very ineffective.

As the days went by, I started to get myself on a schedule. I would always wake with first light and mix hardwood ashes with boiling water for what I called wilderness-coffee. I would then collect any mussels that may have washed onto shore overnight. After that, I would run through the wilderness for about four miles, stopping only to check my snares. I was beginning to be quite successful at catching red squirrels; however, I had a problem. About three out of the four animals snared were found by some other critter before I could get to them. I thought about setting a larger snare around the small squirrel snares but didn't for fear that Aniah might be the thief.

Quickly becoming content with my wilderness lifestyle, I was starting to see myself as a modern-day wild man. I felt that by now, I would probably scare the hell out of anyone that stumbled across me. No soap, no toothpaste, no mirror, and wearing clothes not even suitable for a yard sale, I laughed aloud as I thought about the reaction I would get when someone finally did find me.

"You know, if I set those snares head high, I'll bet that will solve my little burglar problem." I was talking to myself on a regular basis. I think that everyone does this to a point, but I was far beyond that point. "Yes, that may work. I don't see where it could hurt to try. When I check them in the morning, I will hang them higher."

The next morning on my run, I took the time to set nine of my ten traps head high. The last one on my route had been stolen with the catch. I spent the rest of the day scouring the banks for any fishhooks that might have washed up. I considered myself lucky, finding three in all, two good enough to use. With these and some of the line that once entangled Aniah, I planned a fishing trip for the next day.

May/12/89 9:00pm

--I have been here for over a month now and for the first time in several years, I am truly happy with my life. I am not sure that I want to return to society. Tomorrow, I plan to try and catch some fish with the hooks I found today. I also found eight grubs and a few worms by digging under Aniah's leaf bed.

"You know, a fat juicy pike would be good. What about catfish? I wonder if there are any catfish here. That would be nice. Well, I better get to bed so I can get up

68

early, while they're biting."

The next morning, Aniah was waiting for me. "Hey girl, what are you doing?" I patted her bulging stomach, as I talked to her. It was good to see she had recently eaten. "You knew I was going fishing this morning, didn't you? Yeah, you're a smart girl. Come on, let's go."

Aniah followed me down to the water. I cast the line as far as I could, then sat down beside my new friend. "You can tell I'm lonely, can't you, girl?" Aniah panted as I stroked her thinning fur. Summer was close and she was losing her winter coat. I wondered where the rest of her pack was. From my research, I knew that wolves ventured out alone occasionally, but normally they were very social animals, sticking together.

Despite her thinning coat, Aniah was still absolutely stunning. Her eyes were completely mesmerizing. Her build was strong, and I guessed her to be about seventy-five pounds. Being mostly muscle, Aniah was made to destroy. Her instincts to survive would be the motor pushing this force, but in her I also saw an affectionate side. I saw a heart filled with emotion and the desire to love; something very different than one would expect to see in such an animal.

"Bite! Bite! We got a bite, Aniah!" I felt a small tug on the line. With a firm heave, I set the hook then slowly brought it in.

"What the heck is that girl?" No longer in the water, an oddly shaped fish flopped about on the rocky shore. I stood back in wonder. "It looks like a catfish on the front end and an eel on the back. I'll bet you'll eat 'em, won't you, girl?" Running my hand across Aniah's back, she groaned, sniffing our floppy friend. I could only guess what was going through her mind. Maybe her instincts were telling her to eat, but her overloaded stomach was probably telling her that it couldn't hold anymore.

Aniah curiously pawed at the little fellow as I unhooked him. I knew she wasn't afraid of him. I think she was more bewildered by the fish suddenly deciding to jump out of the water and conveniently land right beside us. I was a little confused, myself, with what exactly the little brown guy was. "Maybe a hybrid," I stated, holding him up for a better look. Aniah and I caught two more fish that morning, another just like the first, then a nice lake trout who was bluish green with light spots.

After cooking and eating our meal, Aniah decided it was time for us to play. We wrestled and played tag for about an hour. Then, as if something was calling her, she turned her undivided attention deep into the forest. Slowly walking to the edge of our camp, with her body straight and ears perked, Aniah was completely captivated.

"What is it, girl?"

Aniah turned her head, looking at me for a second then bounced a couple of times, with her tail wagging. Making a half groan, half whining sound, she looked deep into the distance again, then back at me once more.

"You want me to go with you, girl?" I took a few steps in her direction.

Aniah told me in an unmistakable way that she did want me to go with her. She jumped around in an explosive display of excitement when I stepped toward her.

We ran through the Royale wilderness together, taking in the air of deep freedom with every breath. I pushed myself as hard as I could. Aniah, of course, trotted leisurely, stopping occasionally for me to catch up. I was thankful that I had been running while checking my traps, but I was still in no shape to keep up with an Eastern timber wolf. These creatures were athletes of nature, filled with endurance, strength, and stamina.

Aniah led me through parts of the island that I had yet to explore. Ducking and dodging limbs, I tried to keep up. I felt pure, yet wild at the same time. The fresh air, rushing in and out of my lungs, was intoxicating. The lower parts of my body burned from the thistles and thorns tearing through my worn jeans. My legs began to ache with cramps and pain.

"We gotta stop, girl." Leaning over, I struggled to catch my breath. "Yeah girl, I'm in no shape to keep up with you. Look, I've blown a shoe." With my hands on my knees, I stared at my torn and tattered footwear. After a couple of minutes, Aniah energetically bounded about, encouraging me to keep moving. "Okay girl, one more second." I continued to struggle for breath.

We took off again, running into the heart of the island. We ran for a few more minutes, then came to a sudden stop as we crested a small hill. "Whew, I didn't think you were ever gonna quit." I leaned against a large aspen, gasping for air. Aniah and I stood at the edge of a hill, looking over the valley below. Tall green meadow grass swayed, ever so slightly, in an almost unseen breeze.

Small yellow and purple flowers floated just above the grass, while a mix of strong hard woods and prickly conifers outlined the entire area. In the middle, four small brown balls of fur suddenly emerged from the ground.

"Pups! Aniah, you're a mother!" I whispered with excitement. I suppose, being so concerned with my own survival, I had neglected to notice Aniah's enlarged teats. Aniah bounded down the hill, happy to see her offspring. Listening to the whimpering and whining, they seemed even more thrilled to see her. The pups nipped away at their mothers' mouth, clumsily tumbling over each other until she regurgitated a portion of the meal we had earlier. It was eaten for a second time.

Aniah had become a mother in our time apart and seemed overjoyed about it. She didn't encourage me to come any closer and I wasn't going to do it on my own. She was comfortable with my distance and so was I. I had not forgotten that Aniah was still wild and could end my life in seconds, but I still found it very difficult to keep myself from running in and loving on her pups. I only hoped that she would allow me to do so in time.

May/15/89

--I am not sure of the time. My watch has decided to call it quits. It is early morning and I'm starving. I have been sitting on a hillside about seventy-five feet from Aniah's den. She has had four beautiful pups and brought me to see them a couple of days ago. I have not attempted to get any closer. For now, she seems comfortable with

my distance. I have seen no other mature wolves, but I know they've been close; I've heard their calls. I think they know that I am here. I can only hope that eventually they will accept me, as Aniah has.

I sat on the grassy slope for a couple more hours after making the journal entry. The pains of hunger finally overpowered the desire to observe the wolves, forcing me to leave.

My walk back to camp was long and thought filled. "I wonder how many wolves there are in the pack." Lifting my hands with question, I spoke as if I were talking to another human being, face to face. "I mean, it sounded like there were five, maybe six more, calling from the distance. You know, I hate to admit it, but freshwater mussels sound pretty good right now." I continued the conversation between myself and… myself for quite some time, until my life hit rock bottom, literally.

"IIIIIII!" I yelled out, grasping for anything and everything, falling rapidly as the ground beneath me disappeared. It was a hard fall, around twenty feet or so, that left me alive but badly wounded and finding myself at the bottom of an old copper pit; a deep gouge in the earth that had surely been abandoned longer than I had been alive. I was almost sure that my right leg was broken. Numb and tingling, it burned, deeply. "Oh, God!" I screamed out, holding my leg, rolling back and forth. A large cut across my chest bled profusely. Tears poured down my face from the excruciating pain. I looked around, then up at the walls encasing me; walls that were almost vertical, walls that would be impossible to climb. "How the hell am I gonna get out of this?" Gritting my teeth with agony, I blacked out. I don't know how long it was before I regained consciousness, but light had turned to darkness. It was the deepest darkness I had ever witnessed. A darkness that could only be found in the bottom of a God-forsaken pit in the middle of nowhere, in the middle of desolation. A darkness that made me feel more alone than ever before and cold, as though Death himself was just beyond the earth walls holding me. "Help! Help!" I yelled out into the night, only to hear nothing in return. No owls, no wolves, no people answered me. Soon, I began to think about this being the end. I felt helpless. I knew with my leg being the way it was, there was no chance of me climbing out. I sat silent for hours, only grunting and moaning from the pain. I thought about my mother and how she must think that I was already dead. I guess in a way I was... dead to her world anyway.

Covering myself with leaves that had accumulated in the bottom of the pit over an unknown amount of time, I knew that I needed to stay as warm as possible. Even though spring was in season, the nights could still chill to the bone and the psychological side of being swallowed up into the earth on an uninhabited wilderness island did not offer any mental warmth. I lay there for hours, shivering with pain, fear, and insecurity until finally giving in to the darkness. Falling into a deep sleep, even the voice of the wolf did not come to comfort me.

"Tad! Tad! Tad! Tad!" Early the next morning, the

quick rattle of a Canadian woodpecker hammering into a hardwood woke me. "Tad! Tad! Tad!" The bird hammered away at selected timbers, creating a loud resonance throughout the forest.

Brushing the leaves from my face, I looked toward the circle of soft, silent light above me. "Aniah." Aniah stood at the edge of the hole, some twenty feet up. Just as I focused my eyes on Aniah, a shadow moved in slowly beside her. It was the black wolf that had taken her from my camp. This would be the second time I had seen him. The first time his muzzle was covered with blood. This time, I could see the thin lines of faded fur running along his face. I whispered, almost in disbelief. "My god... You are the Charipou. You're the feathered wolf.... the ancient warrior." A feeling of excitement and awe, momentarily, overpowered the pain. Finally, I was able to experience a moment of satisfaction in knowing that they exist. These were the wolves that were once human. These were the beasts that entangled themselves in a ritual, hundreds of years ago, that set them apart from any other living creature known to man. These were the spirits that had been haunting my dreams since the day I first learned of them.

"You can understand me, can't you?" Aniah and the alpha male turned, looking at each other. "No, no you can't. I don't speak your language." These wolves once spoke Charipou, a tongue that hasn't been heard for hundreds of years, a language that had no chance of preservation. They had probably heard my tongue, yelled out as white men ravaged their camps; a language to them of death and destruction. And here, a blood that once sought to destroy them lay helpless at the bottom of an old copper mine. A decision to leave me to die would be nothing less than fair. To watch me suffer and dry up to near nothing would be completely justifiable after what the men of my bloodlines had done to them.

Aniah glared at me with soulful eyes, quiet and motionless. Then, without a sound, she turned and walked away. The warrior followed. "Wait! Wait! Don't go!" I cried. I had no idea if I would ever see them again. As I watched my only hope fade away, every muscle in my body gave up all at once, collapsing me back to the floor of the pit. A sobbing, helpless mess, I was sure that my death was upon me.

Chapter 6
ROT

Three lagging days and nights passed. The nights felt like days and the days like months. The reality of how fragile and uncertain life is weighed heavily on my mind. I came to realize that the only thing certain in life is death itself. Everything else is a gift, whether it seems like it or not.

Delusions began to take over my mind. I saw myself as a small boy back on the farm. I played fetch with my dog, Cricket, right there in that pit. It seemed so real; I could smell his warm puppy breath. He wiggled in my arms and licked my face. We rolled together in the high grass of an open meadow. We chased big monarch butterflies; that is, until we heard Mama calling. "John... Little John.... come for dinner." I could see her in her cooking apron, just beyond the screen of the kitchen door. "Hurry along now, it's raining dirt," she said.

"Mama?" Once again, my eyes caught movement above me. Loose dirt began to rain into my pit at a steady rate. "It's raining dirt, Mama." I held my hands out and

watched the loose, black soil shower through my fingers.
"Mama?" I cried out. "It's raining dirt."

Just then, something sparkled. It wasn't gold, copper,
or silver. It wasn't any more of my hallucinations, either.
A small stream of liquid ran down, splattering across my
hands and face, beading up on the fallen tree limbs that
lay near me. Eventually, it soaked my dirty face. I wiped,
from my forehead, the moisture that had found me. I had
been quite some time without a drink. "That's water," I
stated with confusion. "That's water! Water!" I yelled to
my prison walls, as the trickle grew larger and larger. It
was this single act of such a precious liquid finding me
that brought me back to reality. I realized that this water
was more valuable than any jewel or gem ever known to
man, or any copper that had ever been dug from this pit.
This water was miracle water. No, it wasn't derived from
Ponce de Leon's fountain of youth. It did not come from
the Vatican, nor did it ever fill the cup of Jesus Christ.
This water would quench my dying thirst. This water also
began to fill a filthy pit at such a rate that floating a body
out would be completely possible. It would also be
possible for this body to be dead, or alive. I gathered from
around me the largest of the limbs laying in my cell. As I
watched anxiously, the floor of the pit disappeared
beneath the rising tide. All I had to do now was hold on to
my floats and keep my head above the surface. "How
long, how long will it take?" I whispered.

Two days and two nights passed. I struggled to stay
awake. My body got weaker and weaker. It was taking
every ounce of energy I had to keep myself atop the

wandering wood. The pool of water sucked the warmth from my battered body, making it feel as though my spirit and its fleshly dwelling were just moments away from parting. Hour after hour, I fought to stay awake while the water lifted me higher and higher. Finally, through hazy eyes, I could see the edge of safety. It was within my reach, but two days of spastic convulsing from near frozen body tissue had taken its toll on my strength. I reached forward only to see my arm disappear beneath the murky surface. My body rolled, going under as my wooden supports spread apart, drifting lazily away. Everything seemed to move in slow motion. I felt the cool liquid engulf me completely. Struggling helplessly, my efforts seemed almost useless. My strength was not enough. Just as my body forced me to take another breath, liquid or not, my face surfaced, but only for a moment. Again, I went under. Almost as if I were dreaming, I fought for life from barely beneath the surface. I fought against death for an element that was just above, only inches away. Another roll allowed for air once more. I was only a finger's length from the edge. With the greatest of effort, I reached out then went back under. This time, I gave up. The thought of surrendering overcame my strength to survive. I had no option but to be at peace with my demise. The last breath rumbled from my body, rolling up my face violently in the form of several loud, rushing globes of air. Completely submerged, I reached one last time. I reached with all that was left in me. I reached to find the grip of salvation. I reached to find Aniah.

When I awoke, the frigid cold I went out with had left me. I found myself wrapped with bodies of fur, live bodies, with eyes, ears, and spirits of compassion. Aniah and two others from the pack covered me with living warmth. Opening my eyes halfway, the slight movement caught Aniah's attention. I needed nourishment in the worst of ways. She knew this. She knew that without food, I would surely perish. All the effort, all the digging of the long, narrow trench that had left her and the others with blood-soaked paws would simply be in vain. Within my reach, Aniah opened her mouth wide and returned to the earth a partially digested victim from a previous hunt. The thought of eating regurgitated moose meat would make most people's skin crawl, but my will to survive had returned and it was stronger than death. The vomit of a wolf, the compassion of a Charipou princess, and the heat of friendly bodies stabilized my life-threatening condition for one solid week.

All throughout that week, items from my camp were dragged within my reach. Seven days of recycled moose meat, mucus, and a strong, acidic flavor would grant me the strength to lift myself from the earth that once held me. One week of tender care started my transition into a life that would have no return.

I was finally captured by the wolf that had been hunting me. The spirits that had been speaking in my sleep had now become a part of my life. I was now with the wolf.

Around the eighth day of my rescue, the members of the pack rallied together for an evening hunt. Still wounded, I stopped all doings in the reassembly of my camp and watched the two alphas separate out from the other six adults. The playful mannerism they had been showing quickly changed, alternating between scornful looks warning the others to quieten down, and camp encirclements to check for scents that might serve as an indicator of which direction to travel. No such luxury seemed to be found this time. The pack soon left, falling into a single-file line, as they slowly vanished into the surrounding wilderness. I could not help but to think of how dangerous it was for these wonderful creatures to simply survive. Each meal they sought out would cost a life, and that life could easily belong to anyone involved. I pulled my flint striker from my pack, mumbling the words, "Thank goodness it won't be raw vomit anymore."

With the fire taking, I found upon my ears a beautiful sound. Tonight's meal had been located. I listened for a few minutes as the voices faded into the distance, finally becoming inaudible. Shortly after, the mesmerizing effect of fire drew me in for hours. I began to reflect on what had happened over the previous days. I did not spend any time thinking of nearly losing my life. My thoughts were centered on my rescue. I owed my all to this pack. I was now bound to this family of majestic creatures; bound by a bond derived directly from the love and care of an Indian princess. I felt, now, that I was part of the pack. I would not be left to rot in the bottom of a forgotten pit. Just as the old Charipou chief had been allowed to live on, so had I. John Ryder had been given a second chance. Not only had I been given a second chance at life, but I had also been given an opportunity to run with the wolf. I'd been given a chance at a life most people only dream of. Society may have thought me dead by now, but things were quite the opposite. I had only just begun to live.

While stoking the fire, it occurred to me that the Charipou Indians had stood against forces stronger than I could ever know. There were no laws in place to protect them, only their own ability to fight and outwit the enemy, no matter how great the odds. Just then, the warmth from the flames pushed upward, bringing with it a strange and pungent odor. Immediately, I looked down to check my leg, knowing that if it took a turn for the worse Death could still catch me. "Couggghhugg!" Quickly turning my head, I nearly vomited. One would think that after all the secondhand meals I'd had in the previous week, I could stomach anything. But this was the odor of my own rotting flesh. The look down at my leg had caused my chin to come into contact with the wound on my chest, bursting it open, sending rotten pus everywhere. The pain was excruciating, and the stench, gut wrenching. This was not good, not good at all. As the smell rose on the warm air lifting up from the fire, I turned my back to the heat and looked to the stars. "What do I do now?" Turning back around, I lay down near the fire, then fell into a deep sleep.

It was the next morning when I awoke, well after daybreak, but light is not what woke me. It was the sound of voices, human voices. They were quite some distance away, but I lay as still as possible on the bare ground. It sounded like two, maybe three men. The heat and smoke from my fire were completely gone; a positive, as not to give up my position. Lying on the ground, I looked at my new world with a new perspective. With one eye, I could clearly see leaves and grass with the other, a bright morning sky. I had a decision to make, a very important decision. I could stay here with the infection and possibly die within days. I could seek out these men and be taken back to the mainland for medical attention, returning once I healed. Or, I could go back to my old life and share my short story with the world. As I continued to listen for the voices, my right eye caught a glimmer of something in the grass. I raised my head to find that there were several maggots cleaning up the remains of some vomit that Aniah had left for me days ago. As I started to lay my head back down, a thought entered my mind. "Maggots, they can clean the infection." Quietly, I sat up, taking several of the hungry flesh eaters and placing them directly on the wound. They did not seem to mind at all but continued to work as though they had never been disturbed. Years ago, I had learned that maggots only eat dead flesh, and once their work was done, the infection would be also.

Thankfully, the voices of the men faded. The maggots had helped me make my decision. My life was new, and to go back to the old one would be no different from death itself. The old Indian had seen this same thing, hundreds of years ago. Even though his body was giving out, he did not want to continue to live as a human being; hating, stealing, and owning one another. He wanted real freedom. It is true that, at the time, he did not get the freedom he desired, but by becoming a wolf, he was freed from many of the chains that held him as a man. I began to wonder what would happen to the spirits of the Indians after the two centuries were up. It was then that I thought about Aniah's pups. I had completely forgotten about them. I had not seen or heard any sign of them since falling into the pit. I then realized that I could only be a short distance from the pup's meadow.

--Not sure of the date- watch broken- have been unconscious some- making a guess
June/1/89

--Have had a rough couple of weeks. While on my way back to camp, from visiting Aniah and pups, I found an old copper mine to fall in. As luck would have it, I didn't have my backpack with me, only my journal. The wolf pack actually dug a trench from a nearby stream, which allowed me to float out on some old logs. It's been rough. I have survived on wolf vomit for days now. I heard voices (real voices today), but stayed out of sight. My leg seems to be healing quickly. I don't think it was broken, possibly a badly twisted knee. I hope to be well enough to gather some roots and nuts later.

As I completed my journal entry, I realized that I had made a very crucial error in preparing for this adventure. I had not prepared myself for surviving off an unknown land. I was a woodsman, but I was a woodsman from an entirely different area. Before the incident, my squirrel snares had started to prove themselves. It was obvious that, although filled with hair and sinew, partially digested moose meat could support life. But human beings need fiber. I had not had a bowel movement since falling into the pit. I was suddenly struck with the fear of birthing an oversized child, dry docked. Nervously, I scooted along the forest floor, gathering the greener of the grasses that I could find. After getting a good handful, I knew I had better get myself to a good water supply, make a tea, and force as much down as possible. Grabbing my boiling pot, I hobbled back to the nearby pit that had nearly claimed my life. I followed the trench back, counting as I went, estimating the distance at a little over two hundred feet. My heart was filled with love. Tears streamed down my face. I could never again pity myself for anything that had ever happened to me or that might ever happen to me in the future. The pain and suffering that these animals had gone through in saving my life would be no comparison to anything that I could ever endure.

I took advantage of a nearby limb rotten enough to break with little force but still strong enough to serve as a crutch. I was fortunate enough to find one with a fork that might be somewhat comfortable in fitting the pit of my arm, with a little wrapping. Thinking about the mink that Aniah had given me back in the month of May, I smiled, then spoke out. "Well, girl, I guess this hide will have to be a crutch pad first, then maybe a journal cover later."

After starting a small fire to boil my green grass tea, I gathered some dry grass from the meadow to stuff under the mink wrap. I wrapped it with camp string to hold it all together, then gave it a try. "Not too bad, not too bad at all." I hoped I wouldn't have to rely on such an awkward invention for long, but I knew the more I could stay off the bad leg, the faster it would heal.

I watched the world around me as the tea steadily darkened in color. The steam rising up gave off an appealing aroma, but at this point I still had no idea of what the concoction would do to me. As for the maggots, they were doing a wonderful job on my chest. There were only a few small ones left. I was sure that within the next day or two, these would be gone also, and the wound would be nothing more than a scar. As I poured the stained liquid into my silver camp mug, the sound of a high-flying passenger jet caught my attention. I thought of how these types of things were no longer a part of my world. I thought of how badly I needed to lose touch with the old world and get in tune with this new world, the world of the wolf. I wondered where my place would be in the pack and how I could help in our survival. What could I possibly do, rather than be a hindrance? I decided then that it was up to me to become the best animal that I could be. I had never once, in my life, witnessed a wild animal look up into the sky and wonder about a high-flying jet. I would let this be my last time. From there out, my complete focus would be on nature and my surroundings. I would learn to be as productive of a member as I could be. I would watch and learn from my brothers and sisters, taking from them their skills that enabled them to slip through the wilderness like ghosts in the night. I knew that there would be times I would be left behind. I knew that sometimes I would have to catch up hours after a kill. I knew that whatever the circumstance, it would be in the best interest of the pack. But I was making my decision, and when ready I would take what I could run with, and the rest could rot.

With these thoughts in mind, I tilted my head back and swallowed a cup full of bitter warmth. I could only hope that I was not poisoning myself. I had watched many animals chew on green grass to remedy constipation, and I had to find something that would work for me. I followed the first cup with three more before I started to feel the cramping in my stomach. I filled one more cup, then after a large rolling pain, tossed it onto the fire, sending a hissing steam into the air. I sat patiently, listening to my system work, moaning occasionally from the deep pains. Even through this, I watched the forest around me. I tried to learn from each and every individual that made up my new world. Not just the carnivore, not just the omnivore, but the trees, leaves, and grasses also. I wanted to learn from everything that made up my surroundings. This is what would make me invisible. This is what would make me like the wolf. This is what would make me a mighty hunter and a proud and successful member of the pack. I watched as a small breeze blew, swaying the trees and shrubs in unison. I tried to mimic these movements and thought of how the sound of my footsteps and my movements could be covered with these small but frequent drifts of air. I thought of how an approach from the right direction would help to conceal my scent, then laughed aloud, thinking that my odor hasn't resembled that of a human in quite a while. I wondered what the animals on this vast island might think I was if smell were the only thing they had to go by. I watched birds of all different types and colors bounce from limb to limb. They were far from invisible and did not seem bothered by it at all. Busy about their way, I kept watching, thinking; surely, I must be missing something. Certainly, they had to have some kind of method in place to exist in a world so wild. Consumed by their work, they reminded me of my old life. There had to be something there that I was missing; something they knew and I could not yet see.

The feeling of missing something, with these small birds, was quickly replaced with another feeling. The green grass tea had worked its way through my body and was ready to complete the task. Like any good woodsman, I grabbed my crutch and limped far away from camp. It was hours before I returned, and I was sure my system had been thoroughly cleansed. I felt raw from top to bottom, but the concern of constipation was gone with the grass.

I assured myself that this would not happen again. I did not know what plants on the island would kill, paralyze, or poison, but I knew a method of discovery. I would apply the simple stages of this ancient process throughout the rest of my stay, in hopes of properly sustaining my diet. First, I would mash the juices from the unknown leaf, root, or berry and rub it on my skin. Then wait five or six hours. If no rash appeared, I would put a very small amount on my tongue and wait about the same period. If no problems resulted from this, I would eat a very small amount, waiting again for double the original time. This must be tried with one item at a time, and even if the beginning results were good, the end results could still be fatal. Obviously, I could become very hungry in learning to live or die in the Isle Royale wilderness. Make no mistake, meat would still be on the menu, but veggies had proclaimed themselves a dire necessity.

It was getting close to dark, and I had not heard or seen any of my wolves since the night before. I did not know how far the chase had taken them, but Isle Royale stretches a length of forty-five miles, and they could be anywhere. I only hoped that the humans I had heard that morning had not found my brothers. I didn't know what the men were doing on the island, but they could have very well been there to hunt wolves.

These thoughts made me very anxious to rejoin the pack. I looked down at my leg, grumbling, "You had better hurry up." Covering the remainder of the coals from my fire with dirt, I laid my body on top to absorb the heat. I did not want to take the chance of an open flame being seen after dark. I had not heard the men approach the island that morning, but even worse, I had not heard them leave, either. I really had no idea of their exact whereabouts. As I lay thinking, I decided that I would venture in the direction I had last heard the men after daybreak the next morning. With the rawness, the anxiety, and a few septic-induced outings away from camp, I had a lot of trouble going to sleep. I listened to the forest for the better part of the night, but no sounds came from the sources I hoped.

When I woke the next morning, it looked as though bad weather might be moving in. A deep darkness was overtaking the sky in the west and a strong wind was blowing. I didn't know if the men from yesterday had left the island or not, but I felt if they had, weather like this would most likely discourage their return for the day. After assessing my leg, I decided to take most of my camp gear and conceal it in the thicker woods near the old copper pit I had fallen in. I made a small survival pack to carry with me. Holding to my vow, my journal would be contained in this pack, along with an occupied roll of thirty-five-millimeter film. Everything else in the pack would be essential to survival: string, fire-starter, knife, hooks, Skipper's bow line, and a solar blanket.

Starting toward the storm, my stomach rumbled with hunger. I walked along the edge of the thicket, trying to match every movement with the wind, trying to be like the ghost of the woods. All thoughts were on my movements and the movements around me. I was glad that the breeze was in my face. Not that I could smell the men from yesterday, but it would help to carry their voices to me and also hide my approach from them. It was then, as I slipped past the area where the birds had been so busy, that I thought I realized what I had been missing. "Breakfast." These little guys had been making breakfast. Without a doubt, the nest-robbing momentarily blew my cover, but something so soothing and easy on my stomach was well worth it. I took only six eggs in all, one from each nest I found, and ate them raw while continuing about my way. But I still felt as though I was missing something; something very important that I should be learning from these tiny creatures. I pondered on what it might be for a while, then realized in doing this, I was not at complete attention with my surroundings and was jeopardizing discovery.

I wandered through the wilderness terrain of Isle Royale at a very slow rate. Not only was I a beginner in this world of survival, but I was also beginning with one leg down. One bad move on the edge of a rugged cliff could mean complete disaster. I certainly wasn't as sure-footed as I could be, especially after the pit incident. But it wasn't lack of footing that had almost cost me my life; it was lack of attention. Now, my reduced rate of progress had in turn created an increase in my awareness.

Whispering to myself in my mind, "I only move when the wind moves. I place my feet only where the path is cleanest. Slowly, I keep myself near large objects that hide my advancements." I moved my eyes to and fro, checking in the distance for the enemy. I kept my face to the wind, listening intently. Just as I began to take one more step through the dense brush, I felt a nudge at the back of my leg. Stunned, I slowly turned to see that it was Aniah. I knelt, taking her into my arms, stroking her gently. But something wasn't right. Once again, she wanted me to follow her.

Aniah led me in the direction we needed to go. She did not run this time, as she had the time before. With my bad leg, she knew that I could not keep up. As we continued, the storm that had been steadily brewing

91

worsened. I was beginning to be able to hear the waves crashing against the shore. We continued on, eventually climbing a rocky peak that overlooked a small sandy beach. It was almost impossible to stand against the wind with the edge of the cliff being so high and open. Aniah stopped, then looked down upon the encampment below. Despite the blinding rain, I could see the almost useless efforts of three men trying to hold on to what was left of their storm-battered camp. We watched only a short period, then backtracked fifty feet or so, continuing in our original direction. A few hundred yards later, I saw the first snare. It was of steel wire, similar to my squirrel traps, not made to kill, just to hold. But this trap was large enough for an animal that could bring down a moose or a farmer's calf. This trap was empty, but baited for wolves, smelling strongly of raw meat even through the whirling storm. I pulled the snare closed as Aniah enjoyed the free meal. "Hurry, show me the rest, Aniah." We continued along the path, setting off three more snares in the same manner. Each time, I checked the ground to be sure that I left no tracks of my own. I even stroked Aniah for loose fur to pad the cable a bit. Hopefully, if this thievery continued, these men would get tired of wasting their time on a "ghost" and find a new hunting ground.

"I need to sit down a minute, girl." I had not fully recovered and was tiring quickly. Aniah whined seconds before I heard the voices on the trail behind us. The storm was finally starting to break a little and it seemed the trappers were ready to check their line and get off the island before any more heavenly disruptions let loose.

Aniah and I scrambled to as quickly as possible, continuing on. My heart dropped twice as the next snare came into view. First, one of the younger wolves was caught in the snare, and second, we could hear the voices of the hunters progressively approaching. The young wolf was already terrified and I'm sure my rushing in didn't help. He and I had started a relationship, but under these circumstances his instincts were to kill. After the young wolf aggressively warned me, I could hear excitement grow in the group of men as they yelled among themselves, verbally announcing that they, too, had heard the growling and snarling. I had to take my chances with the wolf, and I had to take them fast. I dove in, shoving the mink covered crutch into his mouth, barely slipping a lunge for my throat. I held him firmly to it while working the snare loose and over his head. As soon as I shoved him back with the crutch, Aniah jumped in. Respecting her authority, he tucked tail, disappearing into the shadows. When I turned to look back at her, she was gone. I quickly scrambled deep into a large rock crevice, just beyond the trap, hoping that the men had not spotted me, but not knowing for sure.

Lying as still as possible, I could hear the approaching footsteps and a strange clanking noise. The lack of conversation between the men made me very nervous. I was afraid that they might have seen me. I could only wait to see what would happen next.

"Well, I'll be a sum' bitch," a large Southern voice growled.

"What do you reckon we got, Tack?"

My heart pounded with fear. I only hoped the response would in no way reflect, "A dead man hiding in the rocks."

"Not sure. I've hunted some pretty smart coon that could pull a good trick back home, but I'm not sure 'bout these here wolves."

"Let's finish the line and get out of here before the next squall. I'm about sick of being wet. We'll figure it out."

"You damn right we will," the man called Tack responded. "You damn right we will."

I hid in the rocks, praying that there were no more wolves caught in any of the other traps down the line. I had helped the only one I could. I did not know for sure what these men would do to me for what I had done, but I was certain I couldn't beat them to the next trap. If there were a wolf there waiting for them, I would know it only moments after they did. The loud boom of their hunting rifle would not only pierce my ears, but also my heart.

A few minutes later, I started making my way back to the high point that overlooked their camp. I stopped, dropping my head for a moment when I heard a single shot fire out. Waiting another minute or so, no more shots followed. I continued on to the high point. The one man left at camp had completely taken everything down and loaded it all into a high-sided aluminum boat. He was waiting on the others. At the edge of the cliff, I lay flat on my stomach, breathing directly into the earth, watching his every move. He scrambled about, completely careless, totally oblivious to the dangers around him. He was not of this world, and he did not belong in this world. He had no inkling of my presence. Another shot rang out, quickly demanding his attention and mine. It held neither of us captive for long. About an hour later the other two came back, carrying a couple of small-bodied animals. From the cliff above, it looked like beavers or possibly river otters, but thankfully not wolves.

Tack, the largest of the three, barked a command, then tossed the dead bodies into the front of the boat. It was then that I noticed what was making the clanking noise. Tack's partner was wearing a belt where the metal snares could be rolled into loops and hung. As these were collected, walking would no doubt cause them to jostle against each other. Tack and the "Clinker" jumped into the boat, while the smaller camp-keeper pushed and shoved, trying to dislodge the bow from the beach. Tack yelled words that I could not make out over the straining engine, but finally the island was freed and some distance was quickly placed between the hunters and the hunted. I sat up as Aniah crept in by my side. Together, we watched the horizon swallow the men up. Instantly, I thought of Skipper and how such a tragedy could happen to someone so wonderful, yet men like these are allowed to live and breathe every day. They do nothing but bring havoc and harm on everything and everybody they can. It's almost like there is something inside of them, driving them to hate and kill, as if it will replace whatever they are missing. As I looked at Aniah, I realized that the Charipou hadn't been released from much at all. They were still fighting the same people that they were hundreds of years ago. Again, I wondered what would happen when the two centuries were up. What did the gods have in mind? Certainly, a lone wolf didn't outsmart the heavenly spirits of the Charipou Indians.

I followed Aniah back into the thick of the wilderness. She traveled slowly for me, but her mannerism was extremely humble as she crept along with her tail tucked. I know that she had to be bothered by the earlier events, as I was too, but with these events, I had found purpose with the pack. I was not proud of that, but thankful. The ability to contribute was a basic and important part of the complex structure of this group. Saving Aniah and disrupting these snares were my first contributions. I could only hope that more opportunities for me to give would arise, but I also hoped that they would not be so extreme and life threatening to the members of my new family.

Chapter 7
BACK HOME

Aniah led me back to the clearing we had visited together before I fell into the old copper pit. As we entered the edge of the clearing, one by one, the other wolves of the pack appeared, moving quietly, as if they were pockets of morning mist gathering from the surrounding forest. My heart pounded with excitement. It had been a couple of days since I had seen the entire pack. I was very relieved to see that no one was missing. Then, I thought again of Aniah's pups. This was the clearing that the den was in, and I was sure of it. I thought it best to wait and see what the other wolves did. I hoped that the pups would hear the pack and come out to play as we all lay down, some fifty to sixty feet away from their earthen home.

There was no playfulness within the group, only moaning and stretching, preparing for an evening nap. The young wolf that had been snared by the hunters came over and lay down beside me. He gnawed at my wrist a time or two, sighed deeply then lazily closed his eyes.

This had a mesmerizing effect on me like nothing else I had ever experienced. There seemed to be a trust, a bond that had been quickly built between us that would not and could not be broken. To have this with a creature so powerful, and so majestic, was soothing, but disrupting at the same time. I knew at any time he could end my life. But I would not give him, or any of the others, any reason to do so. I would only give them reason to trust me completely, and I truly felt that their instincts were telling them no different. As the legend read, "his offspring would posses a spirit and knowledge such as that of his own."

While I slept, my mind flashed back to the area where I first saw Aniah entangled in the fishing line. I saw myself carrying her, as though we were moving slowly through an emerging fog. We moved away from the danger, away from the bloody ground where she once lay. In my dream, as I looked around, I saw each and every wolf's face looking back at me. Aniah and I were not alone. But at the time, I could not see this. Every member from the pack hid themselves in the thickets, cracks, and crevices along the way, watching and waiting. I counted eight onlookers. I could not see their bodies, only their spirits. Like phantoms, like vapors held together by some ionic force, they watched curiously, patiently, sympathetically. They knew, for Aniah, I was their only hope even before I did. They trusted me before I trusted myself. I nursed Aniah back from the edge of death under very watchful eyes. Only the light of the gray moon exposed them. To be like them would allow me the ability to see as they saw. My heart burned with the desire to run with these magnificent animals.

When I woke the next morning, every member of the pack was gone. I'm not sure when they had left, but I needed more healing time on my leg, that was for certain. Saturated with curiosity, I walked around to the front of the pup's den for a peak in. Listening carefully for any warning that might come from within, I noticed no activity. Slow was my approach, but I wasn't sure about how to do this. The thing that really had my pulse up was the fact that any animal inside the den could see out, but any animal outside could not see in, due to the contrasting light. I decided to approach from the side, not to present myself as a harder target, but to let my passivity be seen. Not a sound came from the pup's home as I knelt, placing a gentle hand in front of the opening.

"Psssuuu!" A large red-tail hawk screamed out in the deep blue sky far above, causing me to slip, exposing my unprotected face to the opening. Immediately, I felt a difference on the surface of my skin. At first, I thought it to be a wet sensation, like puppy tongues lapping happily around my face and ears, but as my eyes began to adjust to the darkness of the den, I realized it was something else. There were no pups. It was just the cool air coming out of the earthen home and whatever dirt I might have loosened when I stumbled. I looked into the opening a moment longer, hoping I was wrong, but they weren't there.

Confused, I rolled over onto my back to watch the hawk above. He continued to circle, riding the drifts of warmer air, seeming as though his hovering was almost effortless. "I wonder if you know what happened to them." I spoke to him like we were of the same kind, then rolled back into the opening of the den for another look. This time, I stuck the entire upper half of my body in. It took quite some time for my eyes to adjust after watching the hawk, with the sun providing such a brilliant background. I closed and opened my eyes several times until I was able to see the inner walls of the earthen home. Each time I closed them, I saw the small birds of the meadow, and again, I felt as if I had not learned all that I should from them. In the bottom of the den, dry leaves lined the floor for padding and warmth. As my vision adjusted to the darkness, hundreds of small gray hairs could be seen taking flight every time a breath left my body. Then I found a couple of long, thick brown ones. "That's odd," I mumbled to myself. Scratching around a little more, the smell of death rose up with these small grey hairs. I turned the leaf-covered floor to find a blood-soaked bottom. "No!" I quickly scrambled back, out of the hole. Aniah's pups were not just gone, they were dead. "No! No! No!" I screamed into the wilderness, swearing vengeance. "I'll get you! I will get you for this!" Every muscle in my body tightened with hatred as the bloody mass of leaves crumbled in my crushing grip, falling back to the ground below.

Frustrated, I ran as fast and as hard as my leg would allow me to go. Back to the lookout, back to where Aniah and I had last seen the hunters making their way from the island. I stood at the edge, slinging fifty- and hundred-pound boulders, screaming out as the rocks made their way from the high overlook to the beach below. To me, the crashing of the rocks, one onto the other, was what I envisioned to be the tangled and twisted bodies of the murdering men I sought to destroy. Over and over, I hurled the heavy stones, hoping just one of them could carry with it my animosity. My chest burned as the sweat entered several abrasions caused by the rocks' jagged edges raking against my bare abdomen. Stone after stone, throw after throw, the rage in me became more and more, until my body finally collapsed from exhaustion. I sat on the ground, bleeding, looking in the direction of the last humans I ever hoped to see.

Aniah and the others crept in behind me. I did not have to look this time to know that they were there. She sat beside me with another gift, dangling from her grasp, a river otter. "Thanks, girl." Apparently, she had already come to terms with the loss. I took the limp animal and gently stroked Aniah around the ears. "Let's hope this guy's got some veggies inside of him." I smiled at Aniah, and as does the wolf, I too intended to make full use of everything the small animal had to offer. We then returned to the clearing. The otter, much like the mink in appearance, would make a nice filling meal for me, but it would not replace the anger I was feeling inside.

June/3/89

--I think I've found my purpose with this pack. We were able to outwit some hunters and their snares this

time. I hope they do not return on one hand, but I hope they do on another. Aniah's pups are gone and I want vengeance! I know this is not the way of the wolf, but maybe it is the way of the Charipou. It is definitely how I feel.

I trimmed the bark from every limb that was to go into my cooking fire for the evening, as this would help to eliminate the smoke. While roasting the otter's skinned body atop the flames, his stomach and intestines rolled about in my boiling pot. After cooling a bit, I held the coils of internal organs high and squeezed the steaming, green muck into my mouth. With the open end of the gut touching my tongue, I knew I wasn't eating gourmet, but it was tastier than wolf vomit.

After scraping the hide, I took the brain from the animal and rubbed them together, thoroughly. Looking at my clothes, I figured I had better get started on something new and much tougher. Thankfully, we were still in the warmer months, but time can easily slip away and winter on the island would be extremely cold. I ate all that I wanted of the roasted meat, then extinguished the fire.

It was getting close to dark, and the rest of the pack had been sleeping since our return. Again, I dug the coals into the earth and laid myself on top to absorb the heat. This was very comforting and gave no beacon to guide unwanted strangers. I left the rest of the otter perched on the roasting stick. I didn't expect it to be there the next morning, but if it was, I'd call it breakfast.

Shortly after nightfall, a bright full moon started to

rise into the sky above. It was as if the darkness of night never actually took over, but only visited for a moment, allowing the iridescent moon to make everything upon the earth a shadowy gray. In the minds of most men, being in such a place, everything would seem to creep along, moving on its own, haunting about. With a moon like this, even the trees of the forest could be spooky and threatening. In my transition, I trusted my brothers and their keen senses to keep me through the night. I closed my eyes and joined them in their rest.

In my slumber, I envisioned a great circle of twisted wisteria vines, hovering above me. The hawk I had seen riding the thermals of the pups' meadow was suspended in the center of the vines. Around the edges of the vines were the eight onlookers, who had watched as I first carried Aniah. And as I watched in my dream, slowly, eight faded to seven. My eyes began to fall, leaving the circle of wisteria vines in the great blue sky of freedom. I found my sight directed to the peak of the highest branches bordering the clearing. The vision left as I opened my eyes.

"What's wrong?" I whispered to Aniah as she nudged me with a low growl. Opening my eyes, I realized it wasn't morning yet and we had, at best, been asleep for just a few hours. As soon as I was able to focus, I saw that the other wolves were up and alert, also. Everyone's attention was locked in one direction. Turning, I heard the heavy footsteps with my own ears. Whatever it was had not made it into the clearing yet. It was still in the thicket, and sounded as if it could care less about caution or stealth. A nervousness escalated quickly throughout the entire pack. I assumed that they could tell that this threat was headed in our direction. Following suit, I stood then we quickly made our way to the opposite side of the clearing. We waited at the edge, our faces hidden by the brush, for the brilliant moon to expose the intruder. When she came from the cover, she ran quickly for the meat I had left hanging on the roasting stick. She was quick, but not fast enough to outrun the light of the moon. The haunting glow blended with her smooth brown coat, causing her movements to flow like a liquid-silver wedding gown. On all fours, she stood about four feet high, and looked to weigh around six hundred pounds. She devoured the small meal, then lifted onto her hindquarters, sniffing in our direction. It was then that I knew to avenge the death of Aniah's pups, it was her I would have to kill. But for now, I would have to keep her from killing me.

She let out a bellowing sound as she shifted back to all fours. Aniah and the others met her in the middle of the opening, but all they could do was try to distract her. Thankfully, this slowed her, but this big bear had my scent, and it was my blood that she wanted. I ran as fast as I could through the thick brush. I could hear her crashing and groaning behind me. The small portion of river otter had nothing more than teased her hunger. I knew it was just a matter of time before she caught me, even with the pack nipping at her heels. To her, they were no more than pests, no more than flies swarming about. As I ran, I thought about the rock crevices that she might not be able to get into. I thought about swimming out into the lake. I thought about the old copper pit I had fallen into. I thought about many unnerving things, but then I thought about what it was that I'd been missing with the birds of the meadow; they finally made sense. With this in mind, I jumped for a high branch of a large oak, then quickly scrambled even higher. I took myself out away from the hefty tree trunk onto a branch just large enough to support me. A neighboring tree intertwined with several leafy branches of similar size. Stepping out onto one of the branches of the neighboring tree, I felt that this was what I should do. I was now held between these two points, above the beast that pursued me. Chills shot up my body as her claws ripped into the base of the tree I had just climbed. She was coming for her meal and had every intention of getting it.

"Oh my God," I spoke aloud. For the first time, I was able to look into her face. Any other night and I would have already been dead on the ground, but the luminous, heavenly body that had allowed me to see well enough to make it this far also allowed me to see the wide, glistening eyes and long, carnivorous teeth of the massive brown bear as she made her way up the tree after me. With her lips curled back and the cool midnight air rushing in and out of her lungs, she violently ripped a path toward me. Fifteen to twenty feet above the ground, we were now within just a few feet of each other. I braced myself among the branches of the neighboring tree. My eyes were fixed on hers, but with my peripheral I could see the pack circling nervously below. In one quick motion, she pulled herself snug to the tree then sent claws of strength and destruction in my direction, hoping to knock me from my perch. Her effort fell short by a few inches, which seemed to cause her anger to grow by miles. Again, she swatted with a loud roar, nearly losing her grasp, almost causing herself to tumble to the earth below. She then grabbed the branch I was seemingly standing on, ripping it from underneath my feet, yet I did not go to the ground. In the shadowy light of gray, I witnessed her anger turn to confusion. Perplexed, she held her position and seemed to ponder on what had just happened. After shaking a few more limbs within her reach, she began to rub her face on the trunk of the tree she held on to. The rubbing went on for about a minute, then she slowly made her way down. The pack quickly scattered but remained in the area. From my elevated position, I could see their shadowy figures, circling about. When she had made it to the ground, she sniffed the base of the oak the both of us had climbed, then came over to the tree that actually held me. She circled the area a couple of times, then, as if something were calling her, headed back toward the place we first encountered.

Listening to each of her footsteps fade, there was no doubt in my mind where I would reside for the night. But as the pack reassembled, Aniah whined and scratched at the base of each tree. I closed my eyes and thought back on the clearing. I saw not one, but two shadows in the moonlight. My instincts were changing but were still mostly those of a man. This sow had a cub she needed to check on. She had not given up on me, and Aniah knew

106

this. Aniah knew we needed to put some distance between us and this mama bear, and we had better do it now.

As soon as my feet hit the ground, we ran as fast as we could. We ran in a direction that would only allow us a few miles of land before the great waters of Lake Superior would stop us, but the alphas chose this direction for having the wind at our backs. With the small bear cub slowing her, we were able to expand the distance between her and ourselves. We ran along the water's edge with hope in our hearts and unity among us. We were a tribe of wolves trying to survive in a world that had no laws or boundaries. Each time our feet splashed into the waters of the cool lake could have easily been the last. We did not know what morning would bring, or even if it would come.

When we neared the edge of the island, I again climbed high into the top of a tall timber then carefully made my way over to a neighboring tree, just like before. Despite my adrenaline-filled body, exhaustion was taking over. I took the piece of bow line I'd robbed from Skipper's wreck and secured myself among the limbs. It was certainly not the most comfortable place, but I needed sleep, even if it was only a wink. The rest of the pack laid at the base of the tree in hopes of resting themselves.

I awoke a couple of hours later, as once again an intense nervousness grew among my family. It wasn't quite morning yet, but a light-filled sky was just around the corner. Two of the younger wolves quickly left our encampment, backtracking our path along the shoreline. I could see their shadowy silhouettes against the frothy,

white water that wavered on and off the shallow shore. I
watched intently as my vision was occasionally blocked
by protruding branches but growing ever clearer with the
turning of the earth. I saw them when they charged
directly toward her, showing no fear of death and no
reserve for killing. She, in return, ran toward them with
the same passion. With her small cub only yards behind
her, I watched as the space between them closed at an
intense rate. The rough water beating the rocky shoreline,
just at my back, made this battle inaudible to me. Just
before the sow and the two warriors clashed together, the
two wolves split apart, dashing around each side of the
great bear, showing her almost clumsy. Immediately, they
came back together, side by side, locking in on the tender
neck of the young cub. The three rolled about, splashing
in the surf, while the huge sow tried to bring herself to a
stop. The cries of her cub, although unheard by me, were
heard by her. As she wheeled around to rescue her own,
four shots rang out through the wilderness. Another group
of hunters had decided to join in on the fight, and with all
of the excitement, had done so completely unnoticed. The
shots were the only sounds of the entire event I witnessed.
They were sounds that left two warriors and a small bear
cub motionless on a bloody beach. They were also
responsible for sending a wounded sow crashing deep into
the interior of the island wilderness. The new hunters
stopped their watercraft long enough to gather their
spoils, then faded back, somewhere between the haze of
the morning and into the swells of the lake.

My mind went numb for quite some time.

Feeling humbled and empty over the sacrifice my
brothers made for me, I joined the pack below. I held
them close and cried great tears over our loss. After a
short while of mourning led by the alphas, we formed a
single-file line and slowly made our way to where our
brothers had died. I watched as each member sniffed the
area, circling about. Though I had seen everything, I
could tell them nothing. Their noses and keen senses told
them the entire story, word for word. Aniah left the beach,
walking a short distance into a nearby stand of thick
brush. She turned back, looking at me with a very solemn
stare, her manner changing only to blink. She knew the
sow was just wounded and, for me, posed a more
dangerous threat than ever before. Her normal meals,
even a lousy fish, would be almost impossible for her to
catch. But a man, especially on a pitch-dark night, could
easily fill the empty stomach of an animal that had lost its
edge. It seemed I had finally stumbled onto the real rules
here. They were simple…. Kill or be killed.

Aniah led me and the rest of the pack back to the area
where we had spent the latter part of the night. Black
followed the scent of the wounded sow deeper into the
interior wilderness of Isle Royale. As soon as we returned
to the tree I had perched my trembling body in, the rest of
the pack curled up to prepare for what might lie ahead. I
tried to join them in their rest, but found it impossible. My
heart was broken. I felt the deaths of the two pack
members were completely my fault. I questioned myself
on whether I should remain on the island any longer.

June/4/1989

--My mind is becoming very twisted on who I am. I have two arms and two legs, as does any mortal man, but in my heart I am becoming something else. I want so badly to belong to this pack, and they seem to want the same. I have been able to save Aniah and one of the younger wolves, but two have given their lives for me. I feel I have no family any longer among humans and without this family among wolves, I would not have any reason to exist. Life must have purpose and without that it cannot be deemed good or bad, simply stagnant. I vow to never dwell at such an idle state- to wait upon death without experiencing life- to wait on the end without living.

With the rest of the pack already asleep, I put my journal away and lay down beside them. As soon as I closed my eyes, I envisioned myself moving slowly through thick brush. Startled, I quickly raised my head only to see that I was still in exactly the same spot where I had just lain down. I slowly lowered myself back to the earth, then let my eyes, again, block out all natural light. I could see growths of thick, black crowberry, only feet in front of me, and smell the sweet fragrance of their blossoms. Like a ghost, I moved cautiously through the wild. I could not hear the sound of my own creeping footsteps, but the gulls, kestrels, and other winged inhabitants of the wilderness island called out, making their presence known. It was then that I caught the scent

110

of something that I had never smelled. I held my head
high into the air, breathing in deeply for one more whiff
of the strong odor. It filled my lungs thoroughly and was
exactly what I'd been tracking. When I lowered my nose
back to the ground, I saw my own two front paws; paws
that were as black as coal. Pressed into the soft earth
between them was the struggling impression of the
wounded bear's hind foot. Just before looking into the
meadow we called home, I sniffed a small drop of blood.
Aniah was right. I was in more danger than ever. The
small amount of blood on the trail meant that the wound
was probably not life threatening at all for the bear. But
even after being shot, her quick choice of where to go
made it evident that I was still on her mind.

I opened my eyes slowly to find the rest of the pack
sleeping soundly. The black male had not made it back
yet. I felt I had better kill this bear he was tracking, and
the quicker the better. The more time she had to heal, the
less chance I had of staying alive. The cub had helped to
slow her before, but it was no longer with her. With her
wounded, I had no idea if she or I was faster, and there
was only one way to find out. I removed Skipper's rope
from my pack and gently lifted myself from the ground.
This would be the first time I had ever tried to sneak away
from, or into for that matter, a group of sleeping wolves.
Quietly, I followed the sound of the rustling leaves,
making each step in unison with the wind. Before long, I
was far enough away to make my steps with a little less
care. Eventually, I was in a full trot along the water's
edge, passing the place of battle where my brothers had

111

died for me. I was headed to the overlook from where I had thrown the large, jagged boulders just a couple of days earlier.

About an hour later, I found myself atop the straight-faced cliff. I looked into the distance of the lake for a few minutes, thinking of how I had sworn to avenge the deaths of Aniah's pups. At that time, I thought Tack and the other men were responsible. Now, I knew the truth. If I could kill the bear, not only would I get to avenge the pups' deaths, but I would also avoid the onslaught of mine. I was thankful that I had not yet been given the avenue to the lives of those men before discovering the truth.

I tied one end of the rope firmly to the trunk of a large fir that sat just at the edge of the cliff, then hung the loose end of the rope on a branch, for a quick grab. After scattering several small stones around to make the edge of the cliff as unforgiving as possible, I took one last look at the great blue water that encircled us.

Turning slowly, I crept back toward the meadow. I used the sound of the trees to cover my steps, but I could not figure out, this time, if the wind was my friend or my foe. It covered the sound of my footsteps, but also blew my scent directly toward the meadow, where in my vision the wounded bear lay. On one hand, this could make my run shorter, but my sounds would be magnified in her direction and hers lessened in mine. Trusting my brothers, trusting the Charipou, I gently closed my eyes, hoping for more visions. I could see the meadow. Then, the wind picked up across my back. With my eyes still shut, I saw the great bear rise, holding her head high. Even with the wound, she had no trouble getting across our meadow. Once again, she had my scent. I quickly backtracked within fifty yards of the rope that dangled from the limb atop the cliff. I did not want to get too close. I wanted her at full charge when we made it to the unforgiving edge of the high drop. The powerful wind that had just seemed to betray me almost instantly died down to nothing. It was that that allowed me to hear the rapidly approaching footsteps. My heart began to beat heavily, pounding against the inner wall of my chest. Every muscle about me started to tremble, and I knew that if I did not get control of myself, I would surely be hers. The sounds grew closer and closer, until finally, my eyes caught movement among the thinner timbers. It was Black.

"What are you doing here?" I yelled.

He quickly passed me and then turned back, as if to say, "Follow me, now!" He had no idea of my plan, and I had no idea of his. But a loud roar and crash were sure to let us both know of hers.

A quick glance back confirmed that it was more than time to run and quite possibly too late. I dug in as hard as I could, sprinting for the loose end of the waiting rope. I only hoped it would be strong enough to suspend my weight over the face of the cliff. As I focused on the tiny strand of braided line, I could feel the hungry bear closing in behind me. I continued to run, hard and fast, but my focus shifted. Black stood at the edge of the cliff, exactly where I was to go over. My only chance was to jump over him also. As I grabbed the bowline tight with my hands, I pushed my legs with all my might to clear the alpha wolf's body. It was then that I felt the claws of the great bear tear into my flesh, just inches from my spine. The great bear and I cleared Black together and, also together, our bodies surrendered to gravity just beyond the edge of the cliff. Feeling her claws rip loose as she plummeted to the jagged rocks I had piled so angrily below, I held tightly to the old rope while my body beat against the cliff's vertical face. There was no part of me that did not burn or ache. After coming to a stop, dangling over the cliff's edge, I took a brief look at the bear's motionless body below me, then started the short climb back to safety. Black looked over the edge, watching and waiting. With his tail wagging, he anxiously pawed at the ground above while I made my way up. Slowly, his ecstatic, joyful attitude was replaced with a low, angry growl. He intently focused beyond me. "What now?" I cried. Closing my eyes, I buried my face into the crumbling dirt along the straight. With no light, with nothing but darkness, I could see the great bear starting to move. Almost at the top, I turned back to see that it was just so. I climbed as fast as I could, dragging myself over the top of the cliff. My back burned severely with pain where she had clawed her way in as we went over. Quickly running for one of the larger boulders left on the outcropping, I tried to lift it. With the massive tear in my back, it was much too heavy. I tried several more, until finding one I could handle. With both hands, I held it high then hurled it over, missing her by several feet. While I continued to struggle, picking through the boulders, Black called out

114

with a deep voice, then disappeared from sight. I kept picking through, throwing the rocks, but never hit my target, while the bear seemed to be regaining herself more and more with each and every miss.

Throw after throw, miss after miss, exhausted and defeated, I finally collapsed on the cliff's edge. Just as I would not be killed by her today, she would not be killed by me, either. I watched as she tried to lift herself over and over, doing better and better each time. Then, from out of nowhere, six slender figures appeared. They encircled the great bear, and all together at once, lunged in. In a matter of minutes, all was quiet, all was motionless. The bear was finally dead.

It became evident that it was not meant for me to take such a great hunter as the bear on my own. This would not be the way of the Charipou or the way of the wolf. Our survival depended on each other. A lone warrior against such a great enemy would quickly perish. Two hundred years ago, this is what the old Indian did not want to be. I was fortunate, this time… fortunate to find out that I was not a lone warrior.

We would now be allowed to go back to our home and enjoy the safety of our meadow. The great bear that hunted and killed the helpless pups was no longer. The man-eater that once stalked me would no longer put fear in my heart, but food in my stomach. Her fur would provide me with warmth for winter, and her teeth and claws with tools and weapons. Her bones would grind in the teeth of my brothers for days to come.

June/5/89

--Yesterday we killed the great bear. I took her hide and a large chunk of meat back to camp, while the rest of the pack gorged themselves where she lay. I would have gone back for the skull and claws, but I need rest in the worst of ways. I didn't even wake with the sun this morning; it was probably midday. I plan to go back for the rest of what I want after cooking some of the stripped meat to a good burn. I believe that this will be similar to jerky and may keep for a while.

When I returned to the remains of the bear, I was surprised at how little was left. The wolves had filled their stomachs to the point that they were nearly as wide as they were long. The soft, impressionable pockets of sand told of red foxes slipping in during the night to steal bits and pieces of the unattended carcass. Gulls were beginning to circle and gather about, hoping for a taste also. With the edge of a sharp stone, double the size of my fist, I hammered into the spine just below the base of the skull. In no time it gave way. I held the great bear's head high and gave thanks for the victory. I laid the front and back paws across a large boulder, breaking them at the joints in the same manner. Wasting no time, I slipped back into the wilderness. It was much safer for me to work the hide and loosen the teeth from the isolation of the forest than it would be for me to leave myself exposed to anything, or anyone, that might be foraging along the open shoreline.

As soon as I returned to the clearing, I used the edge of a sharp rock to scrape all the fat from the hide. Holding the fur high, I was amazed at its size. There was no question that many lives had been sacrificed to create such a beautiful covering. I washed it thoroughly, using handfuls of wet sand from the bottom of a small stream near the meadow. The rinsing might not have suited most tanners, but for my needs, it was more than acceptable. I did not consider myself king of the wilderness, nor did I hold any other position of royalty. I was simply a dirty, grimy, unrestrained inhabitant of Isle Royale.

With no way to truly stretch the hide, I laid it out on the open ground to dry while I worked the brains out from the base of the skull. After mashing the brains into the fleshy side of the hide, it was rolled up and placed in the shade for a few hours to tan. Aniah and the others helped in cleaning the brain-mash off once I unrolled the fur. "Good stuff, hey girl?" I stroked her back as she and the others lapped away. I chopped several green limbs about seven feet in length to make a teepee-like structure, then draped the fur over it. Inside, the bottom spread wide, narrowing at the top, making a perfect flue for the smoke to escape. I piled the floor with dry leaves and bark to make smoke, which would preserve the hide and help make it somewhat waterproof. I waited several hours before lighting the fire, to let darkness hide the large, cloudy attraction the process would create. The light made by the fire would be mostly contained within the teepee.

The life of a wolf had grown on me in such a way that

in all my thoughts gathered, over half were spent eluding enemies. The other half was being shuffled between securing food and the visions that were becoming stronger and stronger each time they came. This was the first moment I had found to sit and ponder on the killing of the bear and all that I had seen; the blood trail, the black paws, and the bear's body on the rocks over the cliff behind me.

Besides being battered about, I looked no different than I did when I first came to the island. But were the Charipou gods starting to transfer my soul, too, or were they just allowing me to be a visionary into their world? Whatever it was, it was far from normal, but normal belonged to the old world and I no longer did. I was beginning to believe that my continuing to stay here had nothing to do with Skipper's accident, but everything to do with being freed to find who I really was. Truth is, in the old world, I was a wolf who was an ancient warrior, witnessing by the flame of a fire a student stuck in a cold hard desk; a man stuck in a race that cannot be won but only run until exhaustion and old age finally takes him over. Inevitably, death would've come, returning me to the cold ground I once came from, only for my dust to be scattered about and eventually forgotten by those that I left behind. Taking that path, I would've just been another man who never found his true calling, his true inner spirit. With this pack, with the Charipou, I had found my inner spirit. Although different on the outside, I was the same as them on the inside. I felt the same calling, to be wild and free, to roam without answer to government and control.

There was hierarchy and organization among the pack, but they were unlike those belonging to man. They existed without corruption and were in place for one purpose. That purpose was survival. This wilderness had become my home, and this pack had become my family. I was beginning to feel that I had been called to see their end through. In my heart, I felt as if I might be the last of the Charipou, and the last of the feathered wolf.

With no light left in the sky to reveal the coming cloud of swirling darkness, I started the fire. A sadness came over me as I noticed how anxious the large amount of smoke made my brothers. In just a matter of minutes, they all disappeared from the meadow. My fires had never bothered them before, but this was the first one I had built to create such a thick smoke. I hoped it would be the last. For several hours, I kept feeding fuel to the smoldering blaze, then turned in for a night's sleep. I was still very weary from the days past.

Early the next morning, I woke with no wolves but a beautiful new sky. I was always amazed at how many colors could be strewn across the horizon as the sun peaked over the lake, falling or rising. That morning, I felt like a small boy playing Indian, sitting there in front of my miniature bearskin tepee. Other than the fact that I was completely stranded in the wilderness, it would have been something most boys dreamed of. I took a piece of the meat that I had burned the day before and enjoyed it the best I could. I would have guessed otherwise, but the smell was surprisingly sweet. It was worlds away in texture and ranked several notches above wolf vomit in flavor. The bright side is, if I were here as a food critic, things would be up at least a half-star.

My hiking boots were all but hanging from my feet. Being tied together with lengths of fishing line, I spoke to them directly. "You'll be the first to be go." Taking my knife and tearing what was left of the seams, I laid each piece out in front of me. Placing these pieces on the hide, I used the sharp edge of the knife to trace each shape exactly as it was, with one exception. I needed something to keep the thorns from ripping my legs while running through the forest. The tops of my new boots would be modified to end and be tied off just below my knees. All of these pieces would be held together with thin lashings made from the hide also. With the knife, I sharpened the end of a small but stout hardwood branch, about one-quarter inch in diameter. I placed the smallest of the pieces on the grainy end of a stump and started to drill, with a slight amount of pressure. My plan was to puncture the pieces with the sharp stick, then sew them together as tightly as possible for maximum quality. After about three or four minutes, I lifted the now blunt stick to find that I had in no way penetrated the hide. I smiled as I thought about how the Charipou spirits must be finding humor in my attempts to learn something that they had been doing a thousand years ago. Closing my eyes slowly, I saw nothing. I sat there quietly, hoping for a vision, looking for some form of insight. After several minutes, I realized that I was asking for something much too simple. Thinking that this should be no extraordinary task for a woodsman such as myself, I opened my eyes to find

Aniah. Held in her mouth was the boney, decayed carcass of a small fish that once called the waters of Lake Superior home. The tips of the longer bones protruding from its spine were as sharp as needles.

I reached out with both hands. Aniah dropped the skeleton in one as I pulled her close with the other. "Girl, you are a jewel." I buried my face into her fur while petting her with the love she deserved. She seemed to really enjoy the attention, then, as if she'd had too many shots of rum, she rolled over onto her side to stretch, sleep, and soak up the warm sun.

I went back to work on the bear-hide boots. The bones made punching the holes possible, but it was still a long, painstaking task. Once I got the hang of it, it quickly became the type of work that didn't require much thought. The job was simply to punch a hole about every quarter inch, all the way around, until I made it back to the beginning. My thoughts started to drift as my hands continued to work their way through the thick skin. Again, I envisioned the hawk, circling in the meadow above me. Then, I saw seven onlookers as I carried Aniah's blood-soaked body from the entanglement of fishing line. The birds in the trees appeared, just along the meadow's edge. With the last hole being pierced into completion, the vision vanished. I reached for the larger section that would run along the leg and started the piercing process over. My mind continually drifted, but never returned to the previous vision. I thought about many different things. I thought about my trip to the island. I thought about Skipper. I thought about the

121

coming time when we might have to deal with Tack and his friends or the other hunters who shot the bear cub and the two younger wolves. But when I thought about home, I thought about this meadow and the wilderness surrounding me. And when I thought about family, I looked around at the sleeping wolves that had slipped in almost unnoticed while I so earnestly worked. By the end of the day, I was the proud owner of many sore fingers and one loosely fitting bear-skin boot. Putting it on, I secured the top lashing just beneath the knee. In doing this, I thought of the quick run we had to make from the bear. I stowed all the smaller parts in my survival pack, then rolled and secured the remainder of the hide with a couple of longer lashings.

It was getting close to dark when I reached over to pet Aniah again. "Girl, I hope we don't have to break camp like that again, but if we do, I guess I'd better be as ready as I can." I couldn't help but climb on top of the rolled-up fur and stretch out. "Wow. This feels good. It's a shame I can't keep it this way." But I knew if I did, the civilized side of me would come back faster than ever. In the wild, getting too comfortable is a very dangerous thing. I needed the hide for clothing and warmth, not for cushion. I let my body slide from the fur to rest on the hard ground below. As soon as I did, Black got up and came over, taking my place atop the warm, soft hide. I thought to myself, "He is the alpha," then smiled.

The next morning, I woke at daybreak with no wolves. Breakfast was charchunk, the new name I had given the burnt bear meat. Work resumed immediately thereafter. I worked diligently until the second boot was finished. It looked to be about noon, and no wolves had made it back yet. I was beginning to wonder if I was the only reason that they came back at all, with the pups being gone. The more I thought about it, the more I began to think that was exactly what was going on. It seemed that the pack was periodically coming back to check on me. They could not give up their nomadic way of life. Just as with all packs, they had territorial boundaries and their survival required them to patrol these boundaries. Hunting within these lines and eliminating any trespassers was what provided them with enough food to exist.

My leg was better. It had had enough time to heal. I needed to finish the clothing, and as soon as I did, I had full intentions of joining the rest of the pack on these outings. As I looked at the skull, I knew that it would be quite some time before I could work the sharp teeth loose. I decided that before I left the meadow, I'd bury it and the hind feet and just take the front paws with me. I knew they'd stink as the flesh rotted away, but it wouldn't make much difference with the company I was keeping.

Standing near naked in the meadow, ripping the seams from my jeans, I followed the same method as I did with the boots. The lashings I used at the waist were three braided together. I left the seams along the sides a bit loose for airflow. I knew once winter came these could be cinched tight to hold in more heat, but for now, especially once I started to run with wolves, leaving them loose would probably work best. By the time night had fallen, so had I. I used the last bit of light left to gather some fiber to go with the charchunk. After choking the meal down, I gave in for the night.

The next morning, after singeing the hair from the pants and boots, I decided to walk down to the lake and submerge myself, to help in fitting the new clothes. Not to mention, I needed a washing in the worst of ways. I approached the high cliff with caution. Looking over the edge, there was hardly a trace of the huge bear that had been broken far below just days before. With a gaze out over the calm water, I could not help but find it overly inviting. At the pace of a wolf's trot, I backtracked a bit, then turned onto a path that would lead me directly to the water's edge. As I neared the shore, giving no concern to caution, I ran as fast as I could, diving into the lake headfirst. The feeling was invigorating. I blew spray from my mouth as I resurfaced, splashing about. I took a deep breath of freedom then held it captive so I could dive to the bottom and search for mussels or whatever else I might happen upon. Coming up with a double handful of the tiny, shelled creatures, I held them high and proclaimed them breakfast. After tossing them to the beach, a vision came to me. I looked up to the high point the bear had fallen from to see the eyes of the black alpha. Through his eyes, I could see the lake and me in it. Startled, I also saw a vessel approaching slowly from behind me.

"Ahoy, mate!" the voice of an older man yelled from a short distance.

Not sure of what to do, I hesitated a moment, then used the motion of my arms to gradually rotate myself around and face the on-comer. Faking a Canadian accent, I waved. "Hello."

"You wouldn't happen to be John Ryder, would you?"

I nearly stained my new bearskin pants, that thankfully this guy hadn't got a look at yet. "John Ryder.... Never heard of him. What-, what's the story?" I grabbed the side of his boat as he drifted in beside me.

"Aw, some guy that went missing outta New York a while back. Some teacher says he may be up here. I told 'em for a grand, I'd ride out and take a look."

"You're going to walk this whole island for a thousand bucks?!"

"Hell no! I'll ride around it. If he's stranded here, he'll be on the beach." Slowly, a peculiar look came across the stranger's face. "How'd you get here?"

I paused a moment then smiled, "My brother. He'll be back tomorrow to pick me up."

"Well, why don't you hop aboard and let's have a cold one? Then I can finish my circle around the Isle."

"Can't do it," I grinned. "Got my fiancée waiting on me... she's probably about to tear the tent down right now."

The stranger and I both laughed aloud. I released my hold on the boat as he popped a top then raised his beer high, drifting away with a small devious smile. His engines bellowed out then faded into the distance. I continued treading water until I could hear them no more. Looking up into the forest, Black was still staring down at me. He stood there a moment, then disappeared.

I believe, deep in his heart, he trusted me. But that

same heart had been trampled on so many times. To see me fraternizing with the enemy could have easily induced uncertainty in my loyalty toward the pack. I could only hope that he saw the whole thing for what it truly was. As I brought myself out of the water, I remembered all that he saw. Through the vision, he warned me of the coming craft. Black met me at the shoreline for a drink of the cool lake water, took a look at my new clothing, then vanished back into the wilderness. I had stood so close to him so many times, yet his majestic ways always mesmerized me. He was no simple creature. He was something out of the ordinary, twisted through time, created by gods... once a warrior, now a wolf, and forever a chief. Black was the definition of sublime.

"Tomorrow, old boy, tomorrow," I whispered as I watched the concealing cover of the forest close in behind him.

I sloshed my way back to camp and immediately started work on a small, sleeveless vest with open sides. The hair was singed from this garment also. The only piece left to work on would be the winter jacket. I would have time to do this in the coming weeks. This would be the only garment to keep the fur, and I hoped to find beeswax for extra waterproofing for it. As the clothes that had been water-soaked from my swim in the lake began to dry, their fit became surprisingly comfortable. I rolled up the remainder of the fur and lashed it to my pack. I was now ready to run.

June/9/89

-- I was approached by a stranger today, looking for someone I no longer know. Best part is, he didn't get to see my new pants or boots. I worried about Black trusting me when he saw us talking, but I think he's okay. He came to visit me briefly, afterward.

Chapter 8
LEARNING TO RUN

With my things ready to go, I ate what was getting close to the last of the charchunk and a few roots and leaves that had passed the rash test. My system was feeling more in order than it had in quite some time. I also figured the mussels had helped move things along. I was fortunate to be on the island at a time of year where I was not dealing with these problems and freezing temperatures together. Snow and ice were sure to come, but to deal with fewer problems at the same time makes any transition easier.

Rolling over onto my back and looking to the beautiful bright sky above, I waited for my companions to return. It was at that very moment that I realized how far from ready that I really was. The pack would sometimes kill during the day, but many hunts would be at night. I still had the mink hide from the crutch. I decided that since it was no longer serving as crutch padding, it would now be a day and night mask. In the day, I would look through two tiny slits, blocking out the majority of sunlight, helping my eyes to adjust for stronger vision at night. When night came, I would invert the mask, looking through two larger holes. Leaving the hide full length would also help protect my face and neck from unseen branches and thorns as we ran through the dark forest chasing our prey. I quickly made these four incisions and found use for another lashing.

I sat in the meadow, patiently waiting for my brothers to return. Softly closing my eyes, I could see them approaching in the distance. They were still several minutes away from me as they slipped through a dense section of undergrowth. I knew their location. I had been there before, not in body, but in spirit and mind. I decided I would wait no longer. With my gear on my back and only about an hour of light left in the forest, I took heed of my careless swim earlier and matched their prudence in my approach. I was still learning to be an animal, and I was beginning to see that the hardest part was forgetting how to be a man. This loss was becoming crucial. I—we needed my senses to be as keen as possible. If I were to be sighted in this condition, it would probably turn into the biggest manhunt the world had ever known, blanketing the island with men of questionable natures.

When we got within twenty yards or so of each other, I knelt to the ground and removed the mask, showing my face. As I knelt, the pack stopped, watching curiously. Once the mask was off, they all playfully bounded in my direction. I didn't doubt that they knew who I was, I think they were just wondering what I was up to. We wrestled around on the ground for a short period, celebrating our reunion, and then the alphas led us along our way. We trotted through the wilderness in a northeastern direction with the sun providing very little light. I held my eyes wide, attempting to see the pathway. A blood-drawing slap in the face from an overhanging branch reminded me that I had forgotten to put my mask back on. Using the night side, I managed to get in back in place without ever breaking the pace of the pack. We were probably about half a mile from where we had met up, and my heart rate was elevated, to say the least. It had been a while since I had run the squirrel traps and I was very much out of shape. The majority of the time after that had been spent on rest and recovery from the pit incident.

"Whew!" I blew out a loud breath after another mile or so. Aniah slowed her pace, allowing her soft coat to brush against me. With a small amount of moonlight breaking through the treetops, she looked up then ran ahead, leaving the entire pack behind. I kept running, pushing myself behind Black, intermingling with the others from the pack. They seemed to be ecstatic about my involvement, being sure to occasionally brush themselves against me, as Aniah had, encouraging me to push on.

Suddenly, the pace among the wolves quickened as a distant and mournful cry echoed out from Aniah's soul. Almost instantly, I found myself alone in the wilderness. The pack had found what we needed to survive. I tried to continue in the direction of the sounds but came to an abrupt halt when I thought about my fall into the old copper pit. I certainly did not want to repeat anything like that. I also thought about the bear and how close I came to being eaten, and I probably would have been if it had been a night as dark as this one. I did have some moonlight, but not enough to move safely without the aid of the pack. I decided finding a tree to rest in would be my best bet. I climbed through the branches of a large oak and found a nice fork to lodge myself in. I found satisfaction in the glimmering stars of the night. With no city lights to obscure them, the count must have been around a million. Listening to the voices of my brothers and sisters, they faded in and out of the distance. It was almost morning before I could close my eyes. The adrenaline from running with the pack had me too excited to sleep. I remember my last words, streaming up towards the heavens before I dozed off. "I ran. I finally ran."

June/10/89

--Back on the ground after a night in a tree. I had my first run with the pack last night but could not keep up. I plan to travel in the direction I last heard them, but who knows what today will bring. I do know I've got a lot of shaping up to do.

I swallowed down the last of the charchunk and fitted my mask for the day side. A part of me wanted to run to build stamina, but I knew that it would be too great of a risk. Without the senses of the pack, I had to be extremely cautious. Not only did I not have their keen senses to detect the presence of an enemy, I had little to defend myself with. Aniah, Black, even the youngsters, were quick and agile, with powerful jaws filled with teeth to kill. I thought about the claws I carried in my pack and what kind of weapons I could make from them, but for now something much simpler would have to do. I made my way through the thick of the woods as quietly as possible, keeping my eyes open for any branch that might be sturdy enough to ward off an enemy. Being in stealth mode, I did not want to create the noise it would take to break and sharpen a fresh limb. I continued to walk quietly, watching the woods before, below, and beside me. I stopped all movement as my ears picked up on a small trickling sound. Closing my eyes, I listened intently as a stream was unveiled in a vision. The trickling sound was being made as clear, sparkling water meandered its way through a woven web of branches that all together made up a beaver dam. Several paddle-tailed creatures had together created a small but bountiful home by holding back a stream that cut across part of the island.

"This could be lunch and a spear," I spoke quietly as I opened my eyes. Crouching as low as possible, I used only the necessary movements to make my way toward the sound. When I got close, I knelt to the ground, released my pack, and crawled the rest of the way through high saw grass. Gently parting the tall green blades, I could see the dam just a few feet in front of me. It extended a good forty feet, in a half-circle shape, holding back some of the calmest waters I had seen in a long time. The water itself, skewed with a hint of bronze, reflected the sky and the tall trees around the small pond. The dam

contained enough primitive weapons to start a
Neanderthal uprising. Gradually inching my way to the
edge, my eyes continually scanned the surrounding
habitat for any signs of danger. Detecting no movement, I
continued forward until my hands were wrapped around
the end of a thick piece of hardwood on which the dam
builders had already gnawed at least one crude point.
Expecting the limb to slip from the dam easily, I applied a
small amount of pressure, but nothing happened. I took in
a breath, held it, then applied a little more strength. Still,
nothing happened. That's when it occurred to me that this
limb could actually be a tree, running twenty, even thirty
feet into the dam. But nonetheless, I wanted it. Anxiously,
I splashed into the water, grabbing the limb while
positioning my feet against the dam and heaving out with
a great yell. The first half of the wild cry echoed
throughout the valley while the second half was muffled
beneath the cold water after the limb gave way. Once I
resurfaced, I held the great prize up to find it about five
feet in length. It was no tree, by all laws of man, but much
more fitted for my purpose at this length. I decided to
quickly put some distance between the pond and myself
after my ignorant outbreak. To let out a noise like that
could bring attention from miles around. After a few
hundred yards, I slowed back to a more cautious pace,
continuing in the direction I had last heard the pack.
Obviously, in becoming an animal, I still had a lot of
work to do.

For about three hours I moved through the wilderness,
creeping along silently with every motion. I was starting

into a very dense stand of birch when I decided that this would be a great place to rest and refine the ends of my new weapon the beavers had so graciously started on. As I whittled the cone-shaped gnawings into fine points, my thoughts, once again, wandered. It was so obvious how hard letting go of being a man was. No matter how much I wanted to find my animal side, it seemed embedded in me was a human side, filled with emotional reactions, completely void of true instinct and survival skills. I had to lose this man I no longer desired to be. Closing my eyes, I continued to sharpen the ends into two fine blood-piercing points.

As if it were a fog rising from warming water, another vision gradually came into focus. I could see the pack resting in a valley, surrounded by rocky cliffs. Beside them lay the torn, bloody body of last night's kill. Another moose had fallen victim to the hunger of the tribe. My eyes followed the trail to where their bodies lay. It looked to be about another mile from where I was. Then, with a flash, my vision shifted. My sight was turned back to the path I had walked, coming from the beaver pond. My main focus was directed to a large male cougar that was following my scent. His nose was to the ground, and his pace was quick but cautious. I was, once again, being hunted. Looking back to the pack, I realized that no one was coming to help me. All of my brothers lay resting with their stomachs bulging, basking in the warm sun.

Opening my eyes, I realized that this fight was mine and mine alone. Thankfully, I was equipped with a weapon and blessed with the light of day. I flipped my

mask to the night side. I wanted to keep it on to help
protect my neck and face, but I knew I'd better use the
larger sight holes and not toy with blocking out any
vision. I used the weapon to clear back some of the brush
around me to allow for more swinging room. In my heart,
I hoped that the cat would find my size intimidating and
go on about his way once we met. Kneeling to the ground,
I listened intently, but found no sound. Each time I closed
my eyes I could see him getting closer and closer. With us
now in the same thicket, I opened my eyes slowly. He
stood strong in the trail ahead. He was only seconds away.
I slowly raised myself, holding my arms and weapon
wide. I wanted so badly for this to make him run, and it
did, but only in the direction I so least desired. I braced
myself with one leg forward and one end of the weapon
held low. With a couple of leaps and bounds, he was
airborne. Swinging the weapon up, it was all in vain. The
slow and gawky pace of me against the speed and agility
of a full-grown mountain lion found us both on the
ground with his mouth latched tightly around my throat
and the stick from the beaver dam simply lying beside us.
It was just a matter of seconds before his teeth broke
through the mink hide and our mouths filled with my
blood. I started to panic but then realized how useless that
would be. I no longer wanted to be a man. I wanted to be
wild. Grabbing the animal by the sides of his face,
together we stood. Then together we fell, over and over
and over, bashing the back of his head against the
hardwood limb that once lay passively on the ground
beside us. Time and time again, we fell, until death

overcame him and his tense, violent body became limp and lifeless. Somewhere within the last few falls, I could feel his teeth breaking through the mink hide, pushing into the soft, sensitive skin around my neck. But for him, it was too late. And for me....

It was my first kill.

I finally felt free. I finally felt loosed from the bonds of man. I held the dead body high above my head and sounded out into the wilderness. But this time it was no noise common of man. It was the sound of the wolf. It was a sound no one searching for a lost John Ryder would come running to. I knelt, thanking the Charipou gods for the victory, thanking them for the hide, and thanking them for what would soon be the evening's meal. With the brains already beginning to ooze from the animals' busted skull, I decided I had better make haste in preparation of the hide.

I walked a short distance until I felt safe in my surroundings. After skinning the cat, I roasted the entire body. I quickly discovered that only the meat running along the backbone was edible. The rest was nearly as tough as the hide boots covering my feet. I found a bit of humor as I thought about a way of possibly eating the tougher meat. "Cat-soup," I said aloud. As the smile faded, I decided to just leave the remains for the next passerby. I was quite sure that there were many palates on the island that would not be as particular as mine.

Somewhere in all of this, the thought occurred to me that as the modern world progressed on, so too, did my transition. Once again, I had been the hunter and the hunted. This time, I shared the very dying breath with my adversary. Face to face, we both fought for our own existence. With each expansion, my lungs were filled with the air that had just been expelled from his. And the same went for every breath that he took, until his very last. I realized that in this world, every day for every animal was a fight to make it to the next. Remembering the great bear, I knew that I was not alone in struggling for existence and life was not the only thing that established this. The death of this cat was, however, a test of my strength, a test of skill, an undertaking I had to do on my own accord. With these wolves I had found a place, a family, but I could not be carried. They had been willing and gracious enough to take the time to help me learn to live a new life. In return I had to be strong enough to accept such a powerful gift and prove that I would have enough wisdom and strength to live it to the fullest. An animal such as the great bear would not be expected to be taken by any one member on his own. Even a full-grown moose is a great threat to the wolves, given the fact that any member could easily be trampled. But sometimes hunger outweighs the greatest of threats, and courage pushes the pack on.

With another battle behind me, and a most unusual taste lingering in my mouth, I stood atop the end of a long running ridge that cut through the heart of the island. The view of the wilderness below was breathtaking. I now understood it. Few white men would ever stand still long enough to see this. What the Indian saw were beautiful grasses and flora, rooted forever, flowing with the contour of the landscape, engulfed by a distant explosion of various soft and hardwoods that were freed by gentle breezes to move to and fro. They were accompanied in their seductive sway by tiny buds and blossoms of pinks, purples, and yellows and not broken but in unison with interruptions of large pilings of gray and red rocks running down the hillsides and throughout the valleys below. I could only imagine the wolves, the eagles, and the native fox using these vantage points to spot their prey. As I closed my eyes, feeling the breeze on my face, I thought it possible that the Charipou themselves might have used these very points for hunting or war; survival, at any rate.

Inhaling deeply, the scent of my brothers came to me. Slowly with it, like they were riding a cloud, I could see all of them and their red faces. The fur covering their bodies was matted and stained with the blood of last night's kill. Black turned to look at me. His eyes pulled at mine as though we were in a vacuum. For a short moment, the entire world around us went out of focus. The beautiful valley filled with color, blurred below us, above us, and beside us, as if we were standing still, yet everything else was moving at the speed of light. A few seconds later, we both blinked, and the vacuum was broken. As the vision was fading, I noticed that the other members of the pack had stood together beside the black wolf and were looking in my direction also. I felt a strong pulling force from the entire pack.

I opened my eyes, realizing that I had reached a place in this kingdom, of being. I would find my family as if I were one of them. I would seek them out with my senses, just as they would if they were searching for me. I smiled as a colorful monarch butterfly, with his mirrored segments of black and yellow, fluttered by. He whispered into my ear with an insidious hiss, "I see ye, ole wily wolf. I see ye." He was the first outside of my clan to see me for who I was becoming. I wondered if the rest of the world would now see me too. I could only hope so. I was beginning to realize that it was not the body that made the wolf, a wolf. It was not the keenness or the coat, it was the spirit. With the Charipou, one could be joined into the tribe. The same held true with the feathered wolf.

Scanning my surroundings for dangers from the high point, I checked the wind once again and then started in the direction of my family. Clothed with hide garments from head to toe, I slithered through the thickets and coverings offered along the way. The tiny slits in the mask provided ample vision for movement and continued to wither away at my imbalance between nocturnal hours and those influenced by light. With an occasional breath, I found the reassurance I needed... to know that I was headed in the right direction.

July/4/89

--I've been back with the pack for some time now. Everyone seems to be doing well with my presence. I am very thankful for that. At times, the wolves split off and are gone for a day, maybe even two. Sometimes they go in pairs. We always seem to find each other and reunite as a group without any problem. It's amazing at the excitement they show towards one another, myself included. This is the way it is with each reunion, whether it be an hour or a day of separation prior.

I still had not been able to keep up with the pack on a hunt yet. However, my running and stamina were improving with leaps and bounds. I had been able to salvage scraps from all of the kills and roast them. I tried to do the roasting when the others were away, as not to make them anxious. I guess somewhere in their transition to the wolf, they had let go of the things that were no longer important to their survival. Once, fire, a very necessity to the Charipou tribe, now seemed to be bothersome and unnerving to them.

I attached the cougar hide to the back of my vest as a special pouch for my journal. At some unknown point, the roll of camera film I'd been carrying had decided to call it quits and evade my presence. Maybe somewhere between the bear attack, a fight with a cougar, and hanging out with a guy who was eating wolf vomit, it just made up its mind to seek out better company.

Chapter 9
VISIONS

Since the beginning of time, secrets have been revealed to men through visions and dreams. In the book of Daniel, chapter 2 verse 19, "in a night vision," the dream and interpretation of Nebuchadnezzar was revealed to Daniel so he could save the lives of many. Daniel praised the God of Heaven for this.

In chapter 4 of Job, a spirit passes over him in a dream, whispering words with a chilling voice. In the book of Lamentations, God was angry with Jerusalem and withdrew His visions from the prophets, causing great sorrow to fall upon the land.

Throughout time, many vagabonds and strangers in the night have brought warnings to people across the world over. While some might hold no accord, a select few have been able to accurately predict events well before they ever happened.

In the book of Ezekiel, Ezekiel himself is commanded by God to "prophesy upon these bones," and the valley of dry bones came together and was covered with sinew and flesh. And with another prophecy spoken, the wind brought breath into them, and they lived and became an exceedingly great army.

I was not beginning to see myself as a prophet or a visionary. However, there was, without a doubt, a connection between myself and something much greater than I could ever be. The gods that watched over these native tribesmen, hundreds of years ago, were still here today, still here, living all around us. Before I fell into the beaver pond, there on the surface of the water, I caught a glimpse of my grisly outward reflection. But… I also saw something else. I saw a small flicker, a small shimmer of a humble and decent inner spirit worth having, but only a shimmer, because my transition was not yet complete. There was still too much of me inside of me.

Before meeting Aniah, I was like most other people. My dreams were simply dreams. There were some that lingered on, giving me the creeps for a day or two, maybe even a week, forcing me to wonder if they had some kind of meaning. But after short review, they could be explained away by some inducing advertisement, flashed between segments of the late show. Or by remembering some story my uncle Ralph had told us as kids to try and scare the dickens out of us. Or possibly by the sound of my great aunt farting in the bedroom across the hall while we were at her house for a Christmas visit. Her whole place was hardwood, top to bottom, and the rum always seemed to bring her roaring to life once the lights dimmed.

These dreams, these visions I was having now were

clearly through the eyes of the Charipou. They were not composed of whimsical events, involving singing elephants at Aunt Eda's, roaring lions, or wild monkeys. No one was breaking into my home to try and take my life, dressed in a ski mask, carrying a handgun. This was something of an ancient world. This was something people do dream of and only wish they could be a part of. The twist is... I was.

Closing my eyes, I tried to remember the first vision I ever saw. Instead, I saw a combination of the visions and dreams I had already witnessed, but with a new and added sense. I saw eight onlookers, watching, as I carried Aniah's bloody body from the entrapment of old fishing line. With every step, they were there the entire way, with the exception of one female. Halfway to camp she began to fade. Then I saw the vision of the wisteria vines, but this time instead of the hawk, it was the fading female that was hovering in the circle. I opened my eyes and whispered, "She was killed by the bear while protecting Aniah's pups." My mind went blank for a moment as I stared at the ground. Then I closed my eyes again. In the same vision, my attention was directed to a peak of the highest branches surrounding the meadow. This time I would be able to focus. The last time I saw this was just before the bear attacked, making me run for my life. I could see an image of the strongest tree on the island. High in its branches rested a large nest made by a red-tail hawk. In the hawk's nest were four small wolf cubs.... Aniah's cubs.

"Mama! It's raining dirt," the pups cried. "It's raining

dirt, Mama."

"Get up! Get up! The hawk is coming!" sang the birds of the meadow.

Then a large shadow came before me. "The hawk is the one to give you life. He will give you true freedom." The great bear rose as she spoke, then bowed with grace and honor, disappearing back into the darkness.

Suddenly, in my vision, I saw my own body lifted from the earth, then suspended just above the ground. I was surrounded by a ring of fire and stone and seemed almost lifeless. My arms and legs hung limp as I hovered. Only a tattered pelt covered my groin. Each wolf from the pack came, encompassing me, just outside the fiery ring. In unison, they all sat with their eyes focused on me. As sweat began to weep from my pores, stripes, streaks, and colors began to appear all over my body. The wolves began to chant in a tongue I'd never heard, and their fur changed to flesh; the flesh of ancient warriors who'd lived some two hundred years ago. Suddenly, a great scream was let out, the scream of the hawk. The wolves bowed their faces to the earth before the flames of the fire. I could hear the swooping of large wings, as though they were in a motion slower than time. I began to tremble as the great hawk screamed once more. His body burst into flames as he flew across the circle of fire, hitting me in the chest and then penetrating my soul. The burn was from front to back and deeper in me than if I had swallowed molten lava from the mouth of the greatest volcano. After coming through me, he turned upward, making his way back to the heavens. A rain of fire followed him, diminishing in glow as the embers fell back to the earth below.

The bear spoke once more. "Now you must sleep." I recognized her by sound. I saw total darkness as the last of the embers faded in the pitch-black sky.

In my slumber, I realized that the lone wolf, lurking in the darkness two hundred years ago, had not outsmarted the gods at all. Indeed, the wolf itself had been purposely placed by the Charipou gods to teach the ancient warrior patience and humility. He, the old Indian, was but moments from the freedom he so desired. But his impatience blinded him from seeing so. He was only days, maybe even minutes, from reuniting with the ones he had loved for so many years. His spirit was only a fraction from soaring with the eagles and being with the creator in a way that men embodied on earth cannot be.

But we as men do not always see things for what they truly are.

The old Indian lacked true faith. Faith that the gods were going to take care of him, even though they always had. So to teach him this, they joined him with an animal that possessed a spirit like that of no other. An animal who took from this earth only what he needed, storing away nothing in greed and never killing out of jealousy or revenge. Meek, lowly, and humble with awesome power under complete control, this was an animal that carried with it true faith... this was the wolf.

When I awoke, the world turned as though it never had before. I could distinguish everything around me without so much as having to cast a glance. It was a different me. Remembering my vision, I hastily opened my clothing to expose my chest. I was dumbfounded to find no burn marks, no war streaks whatsoever. "But the hawk, the hawk, he flew right through me." Still holding my garment open, sitting in the dirt, I looked around to find no fire ring and no wolves. I didn't even know how long I had been sleeping. Saddened, I let loose of my clothing and dropped my head.

Then, a voice called from the wind, "Oh one of little faith, stand and see what I have done for you. Stand and search out your brothers."

I stood as I was commanded to do. Holding my arms out beside me, I slowly turned. I could hear the dirt crumble beneath my feet. And in the thickets on the other sides of ridges and even miles away, I could see my brothers, all of them. As I looked at them, they in turn looked at me. I inhaled deeply, letting the breeze carry each and every one of their scents to me. I twirled and twirled about, going faster and faster, until I was like a small child, consumed with laughter.

Dizzily, I came to a halt and thanked the ancestors of the old Charipou warrior. Swaying a bit, I closed my eyes and looked to the heavens. I could see a sky filled with hawks, circling about. The keeper of the flame still had glowing embers falling from his path, creating a long, magnificent stream of luminosity behind him. But most importantly, when I raised my arms to show thanks, it was my arms that I saw. I had been given my own eyes. I was no longer looking through the eyes of my brothers. My transition had taken place. I didn't see the paws of Black or another member from my tribe… I saw me.

The flesh from the bear's front paws had completely rotted away and the joints had stiffened. I lashed one tightly to the back of each hand then closed my fists firmly. The razor-sharp claws protruded several inches past my knuckles. I tossed the stick from the beaver dam aside. A new kind of animal had been born; an animal of many confusions and instabilities. An animal whose worst enemy would prove to be of his own, old blood.

Still kneeling, I tightly rolled the large bear fur and flung it over my shoulders. With one hand, I pulled the lashings tight. With the other hand firmly planted on the ground, I called out to my brothers in their own tongue. Quickly, the canyons, cliffs, and hardwoods sounded back, each without regard, overrunning the other. Then in the same manner, my brothers answered. As life rose from their muzzles, their haunting voices penetrated the wilderness. I closed my eyes, then opened them to a new and undefined beginning. I sprang forward from my stance, racing with a new sense of emotion, a heightened self reliance. I ran, answering to their call, "Come brother, let's join together." As I hastily made my way, the high evening sun burned intently, but could not find me. No shadow was cast upon any ground I trod. I was now moving through the thicks and thins of the forest at an increased rate without putting myself in such peril as before. I was finally free. I could see, hear, and smell danger and prey alike, just as the rest of my brothers could. I understood, in my heart, I now belonged to the clan of the feathered wolf.

Truly, a primordial beast had been born.

Chapter 10
A TIME TO KILL

Fully clothed, using the mask only for protection, I met my brothers on a distant overlook. Through the large holes in the hide covering my face, they could see in my eyes the change that had taken place. They could sense what was now inside of me. My eyes were the windows to my soul, and they now bore the haunting complexity of the wolf. Theirs were mirrored images of my own.

There was little time for greeting among us this time. Instead, the urgency for food overpowered the need for social activity. There was a hunger in all of us that had grown with the crisp cool air that had just found its way to the island. A cold front had moved in, making us want to gorge ourselves with a warm, fresh meal. Add this to the fact that Black had spotted a large bull moose with a bad hind leg in the valley below, and our mouths were watering. It was the reason he had brought us here in the first place.

We split into two groups. Some followed Aniah. Two others and I followed Black. We moved swiftly through the outlying cover, unnoticed at first, but something happened as we attempted to surround our prey. Perhaps a shift in the wind allowed our adversary the scent of danger, or maybe a glimpse of some other treachery in the wilderness spooked him. Whatever it was sent him bounding off into the murky waters of a somewhat shallow slough that had all before sat undisturbed. He stopped as the lower part of his abdomen disappeared beneath the dark water. He knew at this depth the wolves were powerless, yet his strength was greater by allowing the water to lessen the burdened load on his weaker limb. As each member approached the water's edge, he began to sway his giant head, taunting the wolves. My instincts told me to stop just before exposing myself to the moose from the wooded cover that hid me. Peering through the thick brush, I was no more than fifty feet away. It seemed as though I could read his thoughts. It seemed as if he were speaking to the wolves. "Come, come a little closer, that's all. You can take me." He wanted them to attack. He wanted them to enter the slough where, one by one, he could drown the wolves, removing their threat forevermore.

I watched curiously as Aniah and the others paced back and forth, occasionally splashing in, but only for short distances. The moose would simply snort while moving his head up and down. I wondered if he was purposely exposing his throat for these short, inviting moments. I noticed the vegetation that once held firm to his massive antlers had started to sag and break loose. It was a result of being reintroduced to its natural aquatic environment when the moose had first splashed in, making his grand entrance into the pool of stagnant water.

I had thought of this moment many times before and this is not what I had imagined. I remembered how I had listened to the chase from my camp, playing out the gore and the lust of the kill in my mind. I had imagined a much more violent scene. But the truth was, the will to survive was deeply embedded in all of these animals. Even though these wolves knew real freedom would come with their deaths, their will to survive was as strong as any.

I watched the hunger build among my brothers as they continued to pace restlessly about with a feast just beyond their reach. It was then that a subtle change in the wind caused a horrified and unconcealed reaction in the moose. I noticed the foliage concealing my presence move ever so slightly, only to be followed by the swaying of the high grass that stood between me and the old bull. As quickly as the wind made its way across the water, he turned to face my direction in such a manner that he almost lost his footing. The whites of his eyes were wide to see. His heart was filled with fear. He lifted his nostrils to the coming breeze, inhaling deeply. He smelled the great bear. He knew that his death was imminent. The place he had chosen to take his stand would not allow him any more depth. He could only wait. This pool would be a shallow fording for a mature bear and not bothersome at all, as it was to the wolf. The old bull knew this and so did the wolf... and so did the bear.

Sensing the new mix of emotions, Aniah, Black, and the others began harassing the moose even more. He had

151

no choice but to turn back, safeguarding himself from the wolves. I slowly moved backward, beyond the crest of the hill, until I was sure I could not be seen by the moose. I ran quickly, making my way around the back side of the slough, careful to maintain enough distance to provide myself with cover. I stopped to listen to the sounds of my brothers and the moose himself. I was sure I was directly in line with them. Quietly, I crept toward the bank, opposite the rest of my family. There, through the limbs and leaves, like pieces of broken glass, emerged bits of blue, brown, and white as the water continued to be splashed about. Kneeling, I could smell the freshness of the earth as my knees pressed into the rich black soil that had been placed there by centuries of rotting limbs and leaves from the trees above. I loosened the straps that held the hide of the great bear across my shoulders then draped it over my body. With one lashing around the midsection, two around each of my arms and legs, I filled the massive internal voids with leaf litter from the forest floor. I made a hefty looking monster, a grisly looking bear. With the claws still lashed to the backs of both of my hands, I only wished I'd had time enough to add the teeth to my mask.

I closed my eyes to share my vision with Black and Aniah. I saw their thoughts and they saw mine. The rest of the pack would follow their lead.

Resting myself on all fours, I began to sway the brush around me. Intentionally breaking limbs as though they were being crushed by an unsustainable amount of weight, I grumbled deep in my throat, to imitate the voice of the one who once hunted me. Not yet completely revealed from the brush, I started toward the water. The moose began to panic, pacing to and fro, within the confines of his small aquatic cell. Just before I came into clear view, my brothers scampered back into the surrounding hillsides as if to say they had been spooked by the bear themselves. The moose, seeing that the wolves had been frightened off by the bear, was eager to take advantage of the newly unfolding situation. As soon as the last member of the pack vanished from sight, the moose bounded from the water, setting a course for the open ground of the valley. Bad leg or not, his plan was to put as much distance between himself and the bear as possible. It would've been his best bet if there had been a bear. Without the bear, his tactic of entering the slough would have definitely ensured his security and the pack would have given up at some point and moved on. But now, he was on the run, a wolf's tactic. And one by one, we fell in behind him, waiting for him to tire. The pace was set at a playful gait for most of us, allowing the other members to dart back and forth, energetically alongside and sometimes even in front of the old bull. In part due to the miserable hindrance of his bad leg, even I was able to keep up. I had torn the lashings loose before crossing the pond and now held in my clutches the great bear that had driven the bull from safety. It was now nothing more than a long cape of fur, flapping loosely in the wind.

Ironically, the old bull ran the full half mile of the valley before giving out. His race finished at the very base of the ridge, almost where it had started for us. But he was not a meal yet. He was still a moose.

I was the last to approach. Over my own heartbeat and gasps for air, I could hear the moose filling his lungs then blowing them clear, all within the time period it would take most men to blink twice. A thick mucus hung from his lower lip. The wolves started to circle, cautiously nipping at his heels. One would charge in at the front, then one in back. This kept the animal moving, depleting him of any strength he might have had in reserve and allowing him no rest to regain any.

Letting loose the hide, allowing it to drift to the ground before the moose spotted me, I felt it unnecessary to disgrace such a magnificent animal. I started to slowly circle outside the ring of my brothers.

I couldn't help but notice several ravens calling out as they drifted in, perching themselves among the branches of the outlying timber. They were all dressed in mobster black and loudly conversing among themselves while waiting for a table at the island's finest. The faint odor of a red fox told of another scavenger hidden from sight but eager for any leftovers, provided we wolves would be so gracious.

The intense roundabout continued, on and on, until the old bull could hardly stand. He had used his last bit of energy to ward back the relentless strikes of his enemies. He knew one kick from his powerful legs could easily break a jawbone, incapacitating any one of us. But the old bull was starting to show fatigue. Finally, a crucial error was made. His own defenses caused him to stumble.

It was time. The circle could no longer remain unbroken. Aniah flashed across the rear of the animal,

154

passing by his bad leg, then came to a stop some twenty feet away. The twitching strand of nerves and sinew hanging from her mouth led my eyes to follow a bloody path back to the hind leg that had labored so hard in the flight from the bear. With no ligaments left, nothing to support his structure, the hind end of the moose collapsed. While his head was still up, Black lunged in for the kill, sinking his long crushing teeth deep into the throat of the moose. The bull bellowed out for help. This sent a spew of red into the air and a smell of death along with it. He gained no mercy from those who persecuted him. All had their holds now and weren't about to let go.

All held tightly; all but one.

I watched from a very short distance. The anxiety, the passion, and the lust were making my heart beat faster and faster, pulling me in with an overpowering force. The tension in me built as I waited for the perfect moment. Suddenly, the moose rolled, exposing his side. I ran in with all of my might, with every intention of thrusting the ivory white claws, lashed to the backs of my hands, deep into his heart.

It was close to dark when the clan of the feathered wolf began to feed on the big moose. My brothers feasted, gorging themselves with as much meat as their stomachs could hold.

When I awoke, they were all lying around me. My mask was removed and laying near. It looked to be about midday; I assumed it was the next day. Lifting myself from the earth, my initial footing was far from secure. Apparently, my dive in had been perfectly timed by the moose himself. I ran my hand across the side of my face to feel that it had been marked terribly and hurt even worse. A loud ringing was present in my ears and would remain with me for quite some time. I stumbled over to the twisted remains. There was still plenty of meat for me. My brothers had stayed to ensure that the ravens and fox did not rob me of my share. As my eyes wandered curiously along the broken body, my heart filled with warmth. Alongside the moose lay his stomach, unspoiled, still filled with its contents; contents necessary for a digestive system such as mine. It was the only organ left. It was the only one I needed. I fell to my knees, grabbing it with both hands, pushing the mucus and mush from the fly-swarmed sack into my mouth. I came close to vomiting several times, but as the pains in my own stomach disappeared, the smell became less and less atrocious. I sat against the stained carcass, allowing time for what I had just consumed to transform into energy. Within a short period, the restoration began to flow throughout my veins, and my mind reached an understanding of what had really happened.

Together, as a family of wolves, it was our first kill.

--I do not know what time or what day it is. Time is something for the civilized to concern themselves with. It is a way for men to pass the days. I am neither civilized, nor do I any longer belong to the race of men. I consider myself a primordial beast. In truth this journal, this log, means nothing to me as it did before. I gave my word I would keep it. A "gentleman" honors his word. What I am

now allows me no honor in words. I will continue to write so that when my bones are found scattered across this land, the world will know the true tale of a warrior who lived more than two hundred years ago and of those who followed him. I only pray that when my finders lower my body into the cold earth, forever to rest, they will outwardly acknowledge that they have buried the last of a kind... The last of the feathered wolf.

We returned to the cover of the wooded hillside, leaving the open valley and the meal for the hungry below. Spending more time than necessary in the open was not wise for the wolf, and I needed the safety of cover for a small cook's fire. We remained together, lounging in an area that allowed many rays of sunshine to penetrate through the overhanging limbs. My brothers sought these rays out, lying on their sides, stretching and yawning, absorbing the warmth of these creeping circles of light. Eventually, these warming rays drifted away, leaving the wolves to tend to themselves. Many of them would complain with sighs and yawns over having to relocate a scant distance, but as the day gave in, the beams became shadows, casting no more warmth to grumble over.

In the distance, I could still see the carcass of the moose. The ravens were plenty and looked like small black dots from where I lay. I could barely hear their voices, fussing at each other over the choice bites. A small red fox circled about. It was easy to see who had claimed the kill. Each time he would dart in to steal a bite, he was brutally beaked back by the ravens. Their blood seemed thick against the fox, but thin amongst themselves. He finally made a dash in, then headed for the cover of some large boulders. I assumed he had gotten a piece big enough to temporarily fill his hunger. I was sure once the sun went down and the ravens took to the trees, he'd be back for more. I extinguished the small fire just before the coming darkness turned it into a beacon. Nestling myself into my fur, the ghostly cries of a great horned owl drifted across the night air. Another would almost always answer in the distance, and then they would wing their way through the darkened treetops and start all over. It was a wilderness lullaby, my song-to-sleep.

A circle of light woke me the next morning. It tried ever so hard to bring eye-opening warmth to my face but found difficulty in penetrating the thick bear skin as I pulled it higher to cover my head. Mimicking my brothers, I sighed and moaned about having to relocate the upper portion of my body. I lay under my covering with a million thoughts running through my mind. After a few minutes, my eyes began to open. I could feel the warmth of my own breath bouncing back onto my face. As the heat of the sun started to push through the dark fur, my eyes were opened to answer the questions that were going through my mind; had I made the passage? Was I one of the pack? Did I belong here? My eyes were opened to realize that yesterday's injury had put doubt in my heart. There was one answer to all of these questions. Although I was twenty-two years old in life, I had only been born a few days ago. I had much in the way of these animals that had already been given to me, but like any other pup there was still a lot for me to learn. I inhaled deeply, then pushed the cover down as I exhaled. Like the ravens, my breath was divided among itself. Part of the breath remained trapped between the fur and my bare abdomen, staying warm and soft against my core. The other half dissipated instantly into the cold morning air, devoured completely by the chill. It made me realize that we are all but phantoms of time, a short blow in the wind just waiting to be extinguished. Some hearts, like that of the old Indian, would beat for a moment longer, keeping the warmth. Some, like the latter part of the breath and Aniah's pups, would vanish from this earth almost instantly.

I sat up, stretching in the morning sun, to find two of my brothers waking in the same manner as myself. The others were already gone. These two rolled about, playfully gnawing at each other. Suddenly, they let loose of one another, bolted their way under my cover then out of the other side, disappearing into the woods. I was left a bit surprised and cold after watching my fur set aloft from their backs, only to slowly settle back to the ground, far away from my reach. A large smile spread across my face as the two pranksters made their escape into the wilderness.

I jumped to my feet, covered only by my hide pants, while reaching toward the heavens. The air I pulled in through my nostrils told me the whereabouts of all of my kin. Some prowled the wilds in unison, some solo. Today,

I would venture solo. I planned to make my way to the head of the bear.

For the first time in my life, I realized that being by myself did not mean I was alone. I did not know if I would reunite with my family in a day, or a week, but I knew that we were all a part of each other and we needed each other to survive. I knew a lone wolf, without family, without help, would have little chance. How the old Indian did it, I'll never know. What I did know is I was now a member of this tribe and no longer a lone wolf.

And I also knew that if I were ever to have to face the solitude that the ancient warrior did, if I were ever to be the last, without a doubt, I would fall.

But for now, as with all other wolf packs, we had boundaries to patrol and prey to search out. Lacking the agility and experience of the other members, I carried with me a small supply of moose meat, cooked a touch less than the charchunk. It lacked the blackened luster of volcanic rock and the brittle grit of a roasted ironwood limb. The bear meat had been burned until it had acquired both of these characteristics.

My senses, heightened above those of mortal man, caught everything as I eased my way through the forest. I could smell the roots, mice, and moles burrowed beneath the earth as I passed over them. There would be times when any one of these would make a nice filler, quieting a noisy stomach. Above me and beside me, many types of leaves held hopefully to their branches. Every boulder, every rock, each pebble had its place in my new home. There was a new awareness about me, a sixth sense; the same sense that helped define the wolf. This was completely new for me. When I had run to meet my brothers and kill the moose, I had moved with speed, confidence, and intuition. There was a new keenness that allowed me to be more meticulous, more precise, and more thorough about all the things around me. I don't know and never will know if the visionary trait is found among other wolves or just within the wolves of this clan. After all, the feathered wolf possesses something like that of no other. Scientifically, we were all primordial beasts, from the alpha to the omega. We were all unique assemblies, the first of a kind.

After a half day's trek through the wilderness, I stopped for a bite to eat and a bit of rest alongside a rocky overlook I had never seen before. The cover was good, and the elevated view gave me a tactical advantage. Dry grasses held themselves close around the edges of large rocks, and a few pines stood high with their branches starting far from the ground. Many other shrubs and trees rooted themselves a couple hundred feet away, and the wind blew from across the ridge. I put my back to the breeze, knowing that the scent of anything approaching would drift before it, giving me warning. As I downed pieces of the moose meat, I viewed the beauty in front of me. I began to hear trickling water and at first thought that my mind was treating me to a composition directly related to the images taken from my eyes. But, quickly, the amusement turned to awareness when the trickle was interrupted by erratic, bounding splashes. I realized then that what I was hearing was not created within my mind.

Only a fool would allow himself to become so comfortable before checking the other side of the ridge. I got to my feet quietly then made my way to the crest, no more than thirty feet away. Peering over the edge, I found a friend and a foe. Surrounded by lush greenery, the very beaver pond I had met as a man glistened in the sunlight. Its water was a vein of life trickling through our world, but along its edges trotted the feet of an unknown. The beavers toyed with the intruder, slapping their tails at a safe but annoying distance. I watched as the ripples would go out, never to return. The mangy carnivore didn't seem distracted at all by these small wandering waves. A quick meal was on his mind, and he seemed very intent on getting it. Judging by his looks, he had been beaten and starved more than once. I remembered learning in my research that wolf packs would sometimes take others in. But this was not always the case. Coming into our territory could cost him his life. This would be a decision only Black could make.

Any confidence or vitality that the unknown wolf had was immediately replaced with trepidation as Black and two others approached him from the wood line. For a moment, I was filled with sorrow as I witnessed a cloud of blood-stained water expand around his dying body. For that brief period, I thought it wrong to kill your own kind and saw the intruder's presence as only a minor offense. Black, sensing my presence, looked at me from the distance, whispering to my soul, "I am the alpha and the omega. I have seen the beginning, and together we will see the end. He is like the ripples that go out never to return. There is no place for him with the likeness of us."

I lowered my head, hiding my face, ashamed of my contravening thoughts. My leader saw this moment of weakness in me. A feeling of great distress stirred inside of my soul. I raised my head with grief, looking back at my brothers who stood gazing from a distance. I knew I could no longer be weak. I lowered my head, once again, until they all disappeared from sight, drifting back into the thick of the wilderness. I felt unworthy of looking into their eyes.

Collapsing to my knees, sobbing, I knew from then on, I could not question any kill or hesitate to do so. Black's words made me realize there would be no more vagrants allowed in. I was to be the last. After all, the one who was just killed was the one who had broken the bourne.

After getting myself back together, I continued on to the head of the bear. As I neared the clearing that had felt so like home, I was startled to hear voices. I stopped short from sight. At first, it sounded as though a man and woman were arguing, but then short bursts of feminine laughter periodically sounded out; it was a lover's laugh. The sounds grew louder as I cautiously approached. In the open of the clearing, I could see two lovers holding each other, rolling back and forth, wrestling playfully. Often, with their contiguous movements, I would catch glimpses of their brown skin, lean bodies, and long dark hair. Their clothing was scarce, but beautifully adorned. I watched in wonder for quite some time. Perverse thoughts began to enter my mind, as my eyes plundered the exposed areas of the fairer sex. Sexual provocations growled through me, causing me to wonder if there were other garments scattered about and if the rest would soon follow. Secretly, I watched and watched. Several times, I inhaled deeply to get her scent, but the wind did not allow me such a pleasure. It had been a long time since I'd held the scent of a woman, and it seemed as though it would remain even longer. Slowly, the perverse thoughts faded, being replaced with awe and wonder as I began to realize I was witnessing something beautiful, something natural. And just as fast as the sparrow flies, just as quick as time goes by, the beautiful young maiden jumped to her feet, initiating chase with grins and giggles the entire way. Her hair shimmered in the sunlight as it wavered about. Her long, tanned legs moved quickly through the high grass. The man followed, closing in steadily. They were both of great beauty, outwardly deserving of each other and, without a doubt, inwardly as well. I sat quietly, taking notice of how their departure emulated the setting of the sun, only there was no hesitation as they disappeared over the horizon. Listening intently, their voices followed their forms, refusing to employ my entertainment any longer. I tried again for their scent, finding nothing on the wind. It was as though they were apparitions of the forest, merely figments of my imagination. Being near dark, I decided to sleep where I lay. I could take no chances on being discovered and I had no intention of leaving the island alive. I pulled the hide cover over my body as distant thunder rumbled closer and closer, lulling me to sleep.

The next morning, I dug the head of the bear from a

164

muddy grave. It was nice to be back in the clearing. Although we claimed most of the Isle, to me it felt like it was the foundation of our vast home. Before digging up the bear skull, I stirred around for a hint of yesterday's pair. Their odors completely evaded me, but the faint scent of two of my family members lingered about. Unfortunately, last night's rain kept me from identifying exactly who.

The dirt around the head was rich and loose, drawing in hundreds of nice, fat grubs. In the time it had spent subsurface, the short maggot-like worms had cleaned the sow's head of all rotting flesh. The bear, once again, provided me with nutrition. These little nibblets would require no fire for roasting and a half a handful was plenty to curb my appetite. I fertilized the bottom of the hole before pushing the dirt back over, in hopes of keeping the little guys from roaming. This was not exactly gardening, but I had every intention of periodically returning for some selective harvesting. The process, however, was indeed organic.

Walking over to a fallen log, I bumped the skull to free it from any dirt or other insects that might have been residing in it. Two long, narrow centipedes fell from the protective cover, exposing their bright red bodies. A smile grew across my face, followed by a light chuckle, as I reminisced of a time I had performed the yearly ritual of dusting my hunting boots on opening day of deer season. Although only fourteen years of age, I had somehow managed to pull myself from a cozy bed, eat breakfast, and put on my insulated coveralls, all before four a.m.

The only thing left to do was to sit by the kitchen door and put on my knee-high, lace-up water boots. Being of extreme intellect for a fourteen-year-old, I turned the first boot over, softly bumping it against my mom's table. I was careful not to make too much noise and wake anyone else. Almost immediately, a black widow spider came rushing out in an attempt to escape. I calmly flipped the boot over and with a "splat", the black widow turned to black mush. The exact same procedure was performed on the other boot as well, but resulted without surprise. I was satisfied and put the boots on, lacing them tightly. It wasn't until I stood that I felt a twitch in the very boot the spider had fallen from. I became very, very still, concentrating all of my sensory powers to the area of concern, the middle toes of my left foot. Suddenly, there it was again. I began frantically stomping the top of the one boot with the heel of the other. I knew I had to hit the unknown creature hard to penetrate the thick rubber of the boot. Bounding from one piece of furniture to another, clanging and rumbling about, I finally came to rest underneath a garbage can I had, incidentally, forgotten to take out the night before. After wiping off the tuna, onion, liver, moldy garlic bread, and a few other unidentifiable items, I proceeded to remove the tormented boot with caution. By this time, a bed-headed, pajama-clothed audience was beginning to gather at the lower section of the staircase. I carefully eased my foot out, trying not to break any more bones than I already had. Turning the boot over, the remains of a comedian cricket fell to the floor, still twitching with laughter over the prank he had pulled. The sleepy audience laughed along with the bug, then gave a short sarcastic applause and returned back to their warm beds. Needless to say, I couldn't have bought a deer that day, but the skunks and opossums were bountiful.

The fading smile of the memory was replaced with another smile at the accomplishment of the first tooth giving way from the bear's skull, due to my insistent wiggling. I continued to watch the centipedes as their bright bodies twisted their way back into the earth. They were finally where they wanted to be... and so was I.

Chapter 11
THE EFFIGY

It took about as long to finish putting the bear teeth into the mask as it did to finish eating the rest of the moose meat I had saved from the last kill. I was getting very hungry, and another night was closing in. This one looked as though it would be a dry one, unlike the last two. I called out to my brothers but got nothing in return. I did not know if I was being reprimanded for my lack of strength in the killing of the trespasser or if it was just that no one could hear me across our vast domain. Nevertheless, my stomach was growling, and I knew another handful of grubs would see me through. I dug more to the side this time, not desiring to handle the fresh fertilizer I had deposited earlier that morning. In my digging, I found more than food. I found something very special, something cool to the touch that fit in the palm of my hand but did not seem as though it belonged beneath the ground. I carefully wiped the dirt away, blowing at times. As all the foreign grit and grime fell from the object, it became obvious that I was holding a relic of

168

antiquity. It was an effigy, a flat copper emblem that had been carefully etched into the shape of a hawk. An artifact such as this would have probably been worn around the neck of a high clansman or even a chief, centuries ago. It was also evidence that this very spot might have been the predominant camp of the Charipou. What the metal object was made from might have had everything to do with the demise of these indigenous people. Without a doubt, there once was a time when copper was considered more precious than the lives of lesser men.

The next morning, I took the effigy down to the water and washed it off, scrubbing it gently with a fist full of damp grass. The piece grew more and more astounding as the sun grew higher, bouncing its rays of luster onto the golden finish, then back. I was mesmerized by its beauty, but not at all worthy of wearing it. I admired it for a while, then took the shining hawk back to where I had found it and thanked it for what it had shared with me. Gently covering it back into the earth, I fantasized about what it would be like if the piece could talk. I'm sure it held many amazing stories and just as many traumatizing ones, almost inconceivable to modern minds. I would imagine it held tears of pain and tears of joy as well, but I could only imagine.

I was drawn from my peaceful world of reverie by a sound the effigy would not have known in its time. The wind traveled across me, gently brushing the full length of the island. A motorboat was slowly approaching near the high bluff where the bear had been killed.

I quickly ran to the edge of the overlook, leaving the

hide blanket behind. Peering over, my breath ran heavy, rushing by the fearsome teeth that were now embedded in the mask. First the whimpering, then the scent, then the sight of three small wolf cubs came to me as I lay flat, scanning the beach below. They were all tied together, struggling about, and much too young to be unattended. As I continued to look over the area, it quickly became evident that unattended was far from what they were. In the brush, about two hundred yards away, on the edge of a small fingerling protruding out into the lake, a hunter settled in, facing himself towards the trio. His approach was extremely clever. He had placed himself downwind from his bait and he knew the mature wolves who claimed this territory would do one of two things: they would either kill the pups or take them in as their own. The truth was, neither of these mattered to the hunter; he just wanted the shot. I closed my eyes to share the vision with Black. He looked back at me with true concern. One of the great hawks that kept the sky above screamed out, sharing his vision with both of us. Aniah was just minutes from the pups, and after losing her offspring to the bear, only hell could stop her. I didn't know exactly which way she was coming from and even if I did, I was a far cry from the forces of hell. I thought about running for the pups, but I'd most likely get shot myself. From that distance, scope or not, the hunter would probably think I was the missing link evolutionists rave about. The one thing I did know is I didn't have time for all of this pondering about, but I also knew where the one with the rifle was.

He was simply a man. On the inside, I had no idea what stirred his soul. I could only see him with my eyes, as he could me. His lanky frame did not offer much in giving him away, nor did his lack in height. An old camouflage hat and dark glasses helped to conceal him even further. He was without a doubt a stealthy hunter.

I ran to his place of concealment as fast as I could. While running, I pulled the bear claw from my left hand, dropping it along the trail. Removing my mask, I held it in my right hand, to hide the claw still lashed in place. I could now smell the intruder, and Aniah. I didn't have much time. I slowed my pace, as not to let him hear my approach. When he was within eyesight, I raised my hand, shouting, "Ahoy!" The man nearly left his skin, spinning his high-powered rifle in my direction, but never actually taking aim. I recognized him immediately as one of Tack's men. He was the clinker.

"Jeezzz, man! You scared the hell outta me." He grabbed his chest, taking a few deep breaths as I closed in the last few steps. "Sorry about pointing my gun at you."

"That's okay. It's not the worst thing I've ever had pointed at me," I replied, faking a short laugh.

"Say, I don't mean to be rude, but you look like shit."

I laughed at the comment from the hunter, who nervously followed my lead by laughing himself after a second of hesitation. "Name's John Grayson." I held my hand out, inviting a shake. "I'm sure I do... look rough. I've always wanted to come and camp here for a couple of months and finally got my chance. I'm about ready to pack it up, though. How about you? What are you doing out here?"

"I'm a wolf hunter," he growled, showing his teeth and then laughing with a little more comfort than before. "You just can see 'em from here, without looking through my rifle scope," he pointed across the water at the three wolf pups. "I've got some bait over there. The only question is, will they kill them or take them as their own?"

"You can shoot that far?" Aniah appeared on the bank, throwing all caution to the wind, the moment I asked my question.

The man started lifting his rifle slowly to his shoulder, then moved the safety to the firing position. It seemed he also had intentions to impress me. I had no intentions, only instinct. "Well, well, well. You just watch this, mister... what was it?"

"Ryder... John Ryder."

The hunter paused for a moment, then jerked his head toward me, allowing the muzzle of the gun to point into the air. "You're worth ten thousand dollars!"

With a solemn stare, I let the mask drop, responding, "I guess I'm your wolf then."

A single shot rang out just before I let his lifeless body collapse to the ground. He was completely eviscerated. After one swipe and several thrusts, his heart and lungs were lacerated to the point of being almost unidentifiable. They had relinquished their normal positions, falling lower into the cavity that once held his intestines. I stood over him, staring into his dying eyes for quite some time. The way I saw it, he was already dead.

The Holy Bible says, "It is appointed unto man, once to die." Today, he was neither early nor late for his scheduled event, but rather, dead on time.

Once again, the growling sound of a motorboat pulled me back from a situation that completely consumed me. I looked back to the distant beach. Aniah was gone, but the pups were still there. The shot had frightened her away. As I walked from the dead body, I realized it was my first kill…. of my old kind, anyway.

With the onsetting reality, my pace quickened. Without losing stride, I placed the mask back where it belonged, grasped the discarded claw from the forest floor, lashed it to my blood-soaked hand, and continued to run swiftly through the wilderness. The other members of my clan joined in a short way into my run. The smell of the blood seemed to excite them, as we continued to quickly expand the distance between us and the deceased. Or perhaps it wasn't the scent of blood at all; it could have been the fact that I had just broken a boundary I was too "civilized" to even approach only days before. Black had shown me the truth. Neither that man nor any other wolves had any place with the likes of us. I had now accepted that truth.

About a half-mile into our run, a somewhat familiar voice blasted through the wild. "I'm gonna hunt you down and kill you, you damn grizzly!"

Another shouted something after him, but I couldn't make out the words. What I could make out is these men were after me, only in their minds, I was a man-eating bear.

We settled down about a mile and a half from the kill site after pressing deep into the interior of the island. The younger wolves were fervid in cleaning away the fresh blood splattered about my body. I moved my tongue forward to moisten my lips after the hard run, only to find the flavor of human life dripping from the fierce-looking teeth that preceded me.

I must admit, I found the taste… exciting.

I knew Tack meant what he said, but I wasn't the least bit bothered by it. I think one has to see himself as perishable to know fear. I now saw myself as the way scientists describe matter. They say matter cannot be destroyed, only changed from one form to another. I had been changed from a man to a wolf and no longer knew true fear. The things I did know were for self-preservation.

And for killing… my heart no longer felt remorse. The wolf taught me this.

The younger wolves of the group were finally satisfied with their cleaning efforts. Only a few light pink stains were left. They smelled strong and felt sticky, but I knew this would wear off in time. Due to the wind, it was impossible for me to tell if the boat of men had left yet. I was almost certain it had and felt that it was too close to dark for any of them to return. I looked up from my surrounding of wolves to find the sky crystal clear. I could tell it was definitely going to be a cold night, especially if the wind continued to blow like it was. By the sound of my stomach and of a few others around me, I wasn't the only one in need of a meal. We all lounged a bit longer, then Aniah and Black left us to see what the wilderness might have to offer. As they trotted off, I hoped they would turn in the direction of my hide blanket. It had just dawned on me that I'd left it in the clearing. Unfortunately, they did not go that way, promising the coming night would be even colder.

Aniah and Black were back after a short period. I could smell blood in their breath, a scent that resembled that of our own; strangely, a wolf's blood. After a moment, I thought of the three pups the hunter was using for bait. If only he were alive, the hunter would now have his answer. I'm sure he did not intend for things to turn out the way they did. He had had no idea what he'd been up against.

--I slept good last night. I did not know if my conscience would bother me or not, but truly it didn't. I was able to save the life of a beautiful princess by taking the life of another. What is one man's life compared to Aniah's?

I had an advantage over the rest of the pack. A concealment that none of the others possessed. Outwardly, I resembled our greatest enemy, but on the inside we all knew the truth. This appearance allowed me to slip in with the greatest of stealth. No shift in the wind, no noise, no lack of cover could give me away. I only had to fake some bullshit smile and maybe conjure up some tale of the same caliber and my tribe could depend on me to fight the enemy from within. I was the "Trojan Horse"

of Isle Royale. I was becoming more deadly than any
other animal that had ever inhabited the island.

I knew soon, this wilderness would be currycombed
for the man-eater. Not just one, but many boats would dig
their bows into the shores of Isle Royale looking for the
bear. I only hoped that my family would not suffer for my
actions. But looking at Aniah, I wouldn't change
anything, even if I could.

--I killed a man yesterday and it is good with my soul.
He was a bad man, and it was his own actions that caused
him his loss. I will go to the beaver pond now and hide the
blood-stained claw. I feel that tracking dogs will be
arriving soon and they will be able to follow my scent,
any trace of the dead man, or any parts of the bear.

When I got to the beaver dam, that's just what it was,
a damn beaver dam. There was no water to really speak
of, only a trickling stream, no pond, and definitely no
beavers. There wasn't any hope of me swimming down to
the deepest parts to lodge the murder weapon between the
dam's twisted limbs for safe keeping. There was no hope
for me to do that at all. I stood silent, listening to the boats
approach in the distance. With a feeling of defeat, I closed
my eyes to share the sight of my brothers. Thankfully,
they were already headed for the heart of the island. They
were taking them to the bogs, if the dogs so chose to
follow.

That's when it hit me. If the tracking dogs decided to
follow the scent of the dead man's blood, the wolves who

had been so happy to clean the bear claw yesterday might be in great danger today.

Closing my eyes again, I took the vision of the ever-present hawk. Three hounds roared onto the island. Ten armed men followed, as the dogs led them to last night's bedding ground. I would not be able to tell which way they would go until they reached this point. I did not know if they would come after me or if they would go after my brothers.

Strapping the weapon back in place, I put my mask on and knelt to the ground. With my eyes closed tightly, I could see the place I needed to make my stand. It was a bog so thick, so dense with growth, that no man within his right mind would enter in search of a man-eating bear. The long voices of the hounds echoed through the wilderness, again and again, while I ran at my best. The Charipou gods showed me where I needed to be, but it was on me to get there. If I did not make it, I knew the results would be devastating.

The hawk above shared his vision with me in every turn, every climb, and every stumble along the way. Ignoring all paths of ease, this was the quickest way. I was expected to push myself beyond my limits for the preservation of my brothers, just as they had done so many times for me. Several times, I heard the hounds bawl out through the standing timbers of Isle Royale. The hawk showed them pulling tightly at the ropes, held by men. I could also see myself nearing my destination. I would be just in time to make my stand.

I entered the bog of thick growth and mud, crossing a

177

fallen log. This would hide my tracks. I wanted the
hunters to believe that there was a bear in this thick,
nearly impenetrable section of marsh, not John Ryder. A
pool of stagnant water, just over waist deep, awaited my
arrival. This is where I would soon meet three blue-eyed
cur-hounds.

The voices of the men, the clumsy clamoring of
twenty rubber boots all moving at once, slowly bled into
earshot, joining the wailing of the dogs. I stood silent,
hidden away in a natural wonder, wondering if they
would send in one, two, or all three of the hounds at the
same time.

The voice of the dogs changed. They changed to a
different call; what some refer to as "treed." I was treed.
The great man-eater had been treed. I was locked into one
area by these magnificent hounds. Though they could not
see me, they could tell by their senses that I was there.
And by changing the way they barked, they were telling
their masters just that.

The men shuffled about at the edge of the thicket. The
ten, along with the dogs, silenced themselves as the hawk
above shared his vision with me. They were leveling their
high-caliber firearms, not taking aim at anything in
particular, but readying themselves to blast away into the
bog in hopes of killing its deadly inhabitant. Submerging
myself below the murky water, I could hear the many
shots tearing through the brush above. Fortunately, the
onslaught ended before my body demanded another
breath of air.

The dogs, once again, loudly insisted that a bear was

still in the thicket, while the men jabbered about, reloading their weapons. The vile stench of swamp mud was replaced with a smell of sulfur and burnt gunpowder, an odor most people only witness in the form of exploding fireworks.

Again, the men quieted. It seemed a decision had been made. It was then that I made a decision also. Removing my mask, I held it tightly in my left hand. As soon as I heard the thick underbrush giving way to the forceful entry of the dogs, I went back under, leaving the mask to float along the surface of the water. Three bodies came into the bog at once. Together, they swam to the mask. It smelled very much like what they had been tracking. Little did they know how close it actually was. The dogs never really knew what happened. When I surfaced, the claw on my right hand was once again blood-soaked. The larger of the three hounds still had a grip on the mask I had lured them in with. I pushed her away gently as death slowly loosened her grasp. The three, close together, gave in to the pull of the water, eventually disappearing beneath the murk.

It was then that the same yellow and black monarch, who had seen me as the "ole wily wolf," fluttered into the bog with more words of wisdom. He whispered this time, with a sense of urgency, "Run, ye' ole wolf! Run!"

Leaving the thick growth with my lungs pounding as fast as my heart, I could hear one of the men screaming into the wilderness. As he splashed through the bloody water, his heart was breaking. Soon, I would be able to relate all too well to this.

I did not know if the hawk was looking down on him, but I did not care to share this vision. Truth is, I was afraid to. I was afraid that any humanity that might still be lingering in me would create sorrow within my heart.

This was a kill I did not care to remember. It was an unnecessary kill forced upon me by the men who first hunted the wolf and now a killer that was becoming harder and harder to explain or understand.

Enraged, the hunters sent out many more shots, blindly, through the bog. The great bear had taken three more lives, without a sound. It was as if he were a phantom of the woods, an embodiment with no voice, just an appetite to kill. With no trace left, other than the deceased, he seemed to be a master of his trade. But, as with most things, there were perils embedded; the more he killed, the more the men would want him dead. It was absolute, and for the bear, there was no turning back.

Running, my family joined alongside me several minutes after the last shots rang out. They knew I had killed again. They also knew it had been necessary. After all, I was a wolf. My spirit would never allow me to kill out of jealousy or greed. Just as the other members of the pack, I only took what I needed, and I only needed what I took. When we stopped, it was as if we all knew we had reached our destination, but no signal, no sign, was needed. Our hearts roared away in our chest, mine beating the hardest.

I knelt down, embracing the other members of the pack. I held and stroked each of them with a pure love, a real love… a dangerous love.

180

Slumbering there for the rest of the day, we heard nothing else from the men other than their departure a few hours before the sun fell. The moon was nowhere to be seen, but to the eye of the wolf, this made little to no difference. Gazing into the blackened forest was similar to looking onto the screen of a silent movie from days gone by. There was a reflective luminescence. This silvery glow bounced from every object in the woods before coming back to the master's radiant eye. There, everything would be processed quickly and quietly inside the mind of a killer. From this point, simple decisions would be made... And so goes the life of a wolf.

Earlier, not long after stopping at our place of rest, the wind had made it clear that we were very near a potential meal. The alphas would tell us when to act, but for now we would slumber. The scent lingered all night, growing our hunger more and more.

Black woke me at daybreak the next morning. Aniah and two others had already left with the intention of driving the animal in our direction. Black, the other two from the pack, and I formed a line, leaving about thirty feet between each of us. We waited without sound. We waited to hear the brush breaking from the animal's fleeing body, crashing its way through the forest. We waited for what would not come, not to us anyway. The breeze continued to carry the scent of the moose with the added scent of Aniah and the two others. But suddenly and unmistakably, I picked up on the scent of another. It was an odor that my brothers seemed to be completely unacquainted with and I was very confused about. It

181

seemed strangely familiar, but for some reason I could not place it. Whatever it was, it did not seem to concern Black at all. I could not understand his lack of interest. This was not like him. The moose seemed to be his only worry.

All of these smells lingered about for some time, then, as fast as any decision could be made, holding the line was no longer the protocol. We were now in full motion toward the mix, running wildly, without caution.

Cut and bleeding, we arrived at the stand with our hearts pounding. The young moose had made the decision that three wolves would not put him on the run. He was young, but very smart. Perhaps he had seen his mother, or some other, go down by way of the wolf. He seemed to know exactly what the alphas wanted him to do. We wanted him to run and tire, run until he could no more.

The semicircle of three wolves turned into seven. With all of us taunting, nipping, and snarling, the pressure on the moose to flee was tremendous. The excitement in me was so intense, nothing else in the entire world existed. I was living as an Eastern timber wolf, a being in the basics of survival. It was simply kill or be killed.

So caught up in the moment, I forgot my place. Lunging forward, I made an attempt on a very large, well-rested moose. Completely forgetting the way of the wolf, I took a dangerous chance that could have ended in a number of ways. Coming out as quickly as I charged in, I looked down to see a large blood stain covering my abdomen. It was the same blood that ran down my legs and onto the ground below the dying animal. I was more than lucky. It was an unnatural kill by all means of death, but nonetheless, our meal was now falling helplessly to the ground. The heavy load of weighty wolves and the lack of life continuing to run through his veins were sufficient means of capitulation. His eyes were broad and rolling, wide with fear, as he came to the way of the wolf. Ultimately, shock set in, and death quickly followed. No more sounds were made by the moose. Only the crushing of his bones and the tearing of his hide were left to be heard.

By daybreak the next morning, the carcass was completely clean of all soft nutrition. The heart and tongue filled my hunger, as to follow Charipou tradition. I did not eat them as far on the rare side as my brothers did, nor did I eat as much.

Chapter 12
DECISIONS

With each pass of the moon, with each warming day of the sun, I felt closer and closer to the pack. I was denouncing humanity in soul, spirit, and mind. And in my mind, I was beginning to see myself as having the body and full abilities of a wolf. I saw no difference between myself and my brothers other than recognition of the alphas. I knew Black always had been and always would be the dominant male of the feathered wolf. But there was one burning question inside of me. I would forever wonder how long Aniah had been with him and exactly how she came about. I suppose some things are to remain unknown, but maybe his gods felt the same as the God of Adam when he created Eve.

The stains of the kill had almost faded away, carrying their scent with it, but allowing the sentiment of confusion to return. Before the fatal blow was passed, before first blood, a strange odor had risen up with the wind that did not belong. It was an odor familiar to me, but not to the island. It was a smell that had my attention, for if there was one thing I had learned in this world, it was nothing could be taken for granted, and even more so, nothing could be ignored. What had me more confused than anything was that the rest of the pack acted as though nothing was there. But the scent... the scent was definitely there. The more I breathed, the more air I pulled in, the more evident it became to me that the scent was that of a woman, unmasked, natural, and pungent, after days in the bush. I had always thought, until now, that every smell and every sound carried on the wind would be to my advantage. But no longer was this true. I had yet to see her and already I found her distracting. She reminded of my encounter with the airline stewardess, Candance. I also thought of the Indian maiden from the meadow. Then I remembered Aniah. I remembered her in a way that made me hate the thought of being the one who would have to bring judgment down on this woman. But I knew we could not jeopardize our clan. It was as simple as that. And just because we hadn't seen her did not mean that she had not seen us.

-- Again, the hunter has become the hunted. The great bear is much sought after, but this is not what worries me. My brothers' coats are desirable in the winter months, but even this is not of great concern, for now. Somewhere, out there, behind the many trees of this wilderness, hides a threat of a different sort. Is she here to kill? Is she here to observe? Has she already seen too much? Does she know the name, John Ryder?

These were all questions that needed answering in the worst of ways. I found myself disgruntled at the volatility one person could hold in the direction of so many lives. Once again, I had to use myself for what I was, "the Trojan Horse" of my clan. Again, I had to use this human body as a lie. Again, I would be forced to kill... but it was for the good of the pack.

This "Trojan Horse" plan would require complete separation from the rest of my family. The biggest problem I could see was trying to figure out how to approach a civilized woman while looking and smelling like a wild beast. Maybe the best thing to do would be to let her find me. I sat in silence, thinking for hours. The more I thought, the more letting her find me made sense. I would, of course, need to get into her territory. The subtle drifts of wind could help me do that or even the hawk could be of assistance. I thought it would be best if I brought myself upwind of her and let my voice carry down. Maybe I would just pretend to be an innocent visitor of the island myself, singing loudly as I strolled along the rocky shores.

It was a long, lonely walk, leaving the pack, but they understood what I had told them. They knew what I had to do and that I had to do it alone. They also understood that it was for the good and preservation of us all.

I picked up on the woman's scent about a half mile east of the moose carcass. She was moving, not fast, but directly away from us, toward the southern shore. I had to hurry in case her intent was to leave the island. Again, I did not know if she had witnessed my presence or not. If

186

she had, it could bring great harm to my wolf family.

I was not wrong in placing what rode on the wind. It was definitely a woman. At first, I saw her from a distance, struggling with her bulky equipment, trying to navigate through the rough, unforgiving Isle Royale terrain. She was obviously no expert photographer with state-of-the-art equipment. She bumbled around heavy, secondhand junk. I almost started to feel sorrow for her, because she probably loved taking pictures in the wild, but as people sometimes do, she had found herself in the wrong place at the wrong time.

No, I was not wrong in placing her as a woman by the scent that carried on the wind, but after seeing her, she did not remind me of Candance or Aniah. She did not remind me of the Indians from the meadow who I now understood to be Black and Aniah in their human forms. Unknowingly, I had watched them play in wonder just before finding the effigy.

She was thick built, not to the point of being too big, but thick as in muscular; maybe from growing up as an athlete coupled with heavyset genes, or maybe from just wrestling her bulky equipment throughout mountainous terrain day after day. Nonetheless, to us, she was what she had been from the beginning: simply a threat, nothing more, nothing less.

My job now was to eliminate this threat. It would be easy. This was no mountain lion or hungry bear. This was no bull moose capable of crushing a full-grown man. This was not even a man. This was a mere woman, designed to bear and nurture small children. She was completely out

187

of her element, and I had watched her long enough. My decision had been made. I would simply run her down as the wolf does all of its prey. After all, I was a wolf.

I left the high ground at full gait, with both eyes locked on my target. Gripping the claws tightly, the mask flung askew, tethered loosely around my neck, I was moving at a rate that would do away with the open ground between us in no time. My noisy approach alerted the stranger just moments before I was on her. She tried to run but fell into a small rocky depression. I stopped at the edge, grabbing a large boulder. This kill would be much like the one that took the life of the great bear. I would not mutilate her like I did the hunter or the hounds. I would take her life by stoning her. This would bring no more action toward the man-eater from the outside world, but would probably be looked upon as a sad, fatal accident; another hiker overcome by elements in the wild. Many questions of why a single woman would dare brave such a treacherous area alone would infect the news channels of modern society.

Just when I was about to throw the boulder, just when I was about to send it with all of my might, she turned. And the instant I saw her face, her son dropped the stone. All that her world revolved around withdrew his actions.

"John!" She spoke with desperate relief.

"Mother!" I looked upon her face with disbelief. She trembled with fear, too afraid to stand, stuck in the rocky depression. "How... how?"

She started to speak again, with a glimmer of hope presenting itself in her pale green eyes as she reached for

188

my hand. She reached only to be shoved back into the depression by the jaws of death.

A feeling of emptiness instantly devoured my soul. There were so many things I wanted to ask her. There were so many things I wanted to say. But these words would never be allowed to flow between us.

"Black! No!" I leaped forward, toward the two of them, but it was too late. He had come from nowhere, pushing her back into the large encapsulating rocks that outlined the depression. With his mouth around her neck, their dying eyes locked together; hers having only moments to live, his but a day closer to his own demise.

Grief-stricken, I collapsed to my knees with my hands in the air, shouting aloud, "Why? Why!" But deep down, I knew why. I guess my tears of humanity created confusion and for the moment, my face was a river. Out of all the people in the world to actually be able to track me down, I would have never thought it to be her. This was in no doubt proof that a mother's love is stronger than any other.

I turned and walked away, sobbing, as Black dropped her lifeless body to the ground. There was no way I could think clearly, but I knew enough to know that the wolf clan was now in great danger. They would be hunted just like the great bear. It crossed my mind to go back and cover up what Black had done, but the mere thought of ripping my claws through my own mother turned my stomach. We had all become the hunted.

We reunited in the clearing we called home. It was only three days before we saw the vultures circling in the distance, but I suppose the dogs needed no help in finding her or us for that matter. We didn't try to run or hide. I guess we all knew it was time for us to fly. The hawk above showed us the many men surrounding us as we lay just beneath the tall dry grass of the meadow. The flames of fire caught easily, lit from several points along the outer circle, quickly rushing inward with the twisting breeze. Then, the gunshots rang out.

I can only imagine what went through the minds of the men as they tried to subdue me while my family was killed off, one by one. I fought hard against the many men but was eventually beaten unconscious, then tied with thick ropes for the journey back to civilization. Everything I had ever loved lay dead on that Godforsaken island, and, against my will, I was pulled away alive.

When we got back to the mainland, every news reporter, every detective, and every busybody within a hundred miles was waiting. Bright, flashing lights lined the shore. I was rushed into the back of a van, chained, then escorted to the state hospital. There, I was diagnosed mentally ill and was believed to have more than one personality dwelling within me.

Chapter 13
GLASS

I've been confined to this bed for weeks now, poked and prodded with needles and tubes. They have finally found the "humanity" to release the straps, under the strict provision that the door remain guarded and locked. I am thankful, though; it has allowed me time for this final entry.

--I have looked down from the window of this hospital room for quite some time; I have looked down at the sidewalk, far below. The passersby remind me of the ravens back home. Today is the first time I have had the chance to look into a mirror since my transition. I see the weathered face of a defeated warrior. I see the eyes of a lone wolf. As I pace between the mirror and the window, I realize I cannot face this world alone. As with my brothers, it is time for me to fly.
The glass must be broken.

Chapter 14
A NOTE TO THE READER

"I am an admirer and was a person of inspiration to the late John Ryder. I stand in awe of him and his family and what they have endured. Today we… we bury the last of the feathered wolf."

As John's body was being lowered into the ground, I tossed his journal forward. I don't know what came over me. I guess the grief of losing the last of a species was too much. But John's death and the death of all of the others should not be in vain, for he had a want to let the world know, a wish that must be kept. For a moment, I had forgotten how his continued writing was not for himself, but to enlighten the rest of the world of these magical creatures. Just as I realized what I had done, just as my eyes focused through my thin round lenses onto the hidebound book, a great scream was let out. Suddenly, a massive red-tail hawk flew from the center of the sun, grasping the tablet in his talons, holding it just long enough to return it to me, the keeper of the book, Professor Phillip Edward Quartz.

Postscript: But from the shadows of my mind, a lone wolf jumped from all of the darkness I've ever known, catching the hawk, devouring its soul, taking its spirit as its own....

"I see ye, ole wily wolf... I see ye."

About the Author

James Luker, a native of Monroe County Alabama, currently resides in the upstate of South Carolina. He is a college graduate, holding two associate degrees, and works as a multi-craft maintenance technician. Shot twice, run over once, and having survived a physical brain injury, his life has been more than colorful. He enjoys fishing, hiking, sailing, and fast cars; although his wife refuses to let him have another one. He loves to write and is currently working on a prequel to Bury the Wolf.

Find out more at:

burythewolf.com

otisthegoatpublishing.net

and

on YouTube at

Otis the Goat Publishing @otisthegoatbooks

Please leave a review.

Your thoughts matter.

Contact the Author at:

otisthegoatpublishing@gmail.com

James H. Luker